VIR LUCIS

TALE ONE IN
THE LIGHT BRINGERS SAGA

GARY WINCHESTER

GARY WINCHESTER

Vir Lucis

Tale One in the Light Bringers Saga

GPC
GIBBS PUBLISHING
CONGLOMERATE

First published by Gibbs Publishing Conglomerate 2025

This novel is entirely a work of fiction. The names, characters and incidents portrayed in it are the work of the author's imagination. Any resemblance to actual persons, living or dead, events or localities is entirely coincidental.

First edition

ISBN: 978-1-966856-27-6

This book was professionally typeset on Reedsy.
Find out more at reedsy.com

To all my lovely family and friends...

After crushing Caesar's assassins through several brutal campaigns, the Second Triumvirate had managed to bring the Roman Republic several years of peace. Yet, as the Second Triumvirate crumbles, peace in Rome becomes faint, plunging the mighty republic in a bloody civil war once again. And the rising Imperator Octavian, now controls the mighty arm of Rome's army. With his eyes set on Egypt he sends the fleet to blockade the bay of Actium vowing to end the Great Mark Anthony and Queen Cleopatra.

Preface

In the age of shadow, courage is no longer a relic of old tales—it is the weapon and shield of the present. The world you are about to enter is not merely a stage for battles of swords and shields, but a landscape where darkness takes many forms: fear, deceit, and the silent erosion of hope. In this world, the warrior is not defined by armor alone, but by the steadfastness of heart.

The warriors of old did not choose the path of shadow—they stood against it, even when the odds were impossibly against them. They understood that light, no matter how small, carries the power to turn the tide of despair. To be like them is to rise when others falter, to speak truth when lies gather like storm clouds, and to fight for what is right, even when no one sees.

As you turn these pages, remember that every shadow can be confronted, every darkness challenged, and every injustice met with the courage of one who refuses to kneel. Let this story remind you that within each of us lies the spark of the ancient warrior—undaunted, unwavering, and unbroken.

Acknowledgments

To my readers—thank you. Every page you turn, every story you embrace, gives life to these words in a way I could never have imagined. Your curiosity, your imagination, and your willingness to journey into this world alongside me are the true heart of this book. This story exists because of you, and I am endlessly grateful for your time, your support, and your belief in the power of stories.

Prologue

Bay of Actium
  September 2, 31 B.C.

"I have spilled blood and wage war from Rome and throughout its provinces. When will it end? Will I ever make it back home to my family," Cornelius Vesta asked himself, as he stood on the bow of his ship, silently studying the amethyst stone in his hand.

The afternoon sun glinted off the large blue waves which curled and crashed against the vessel. Cornelius continued to stand tall, his red *paludamentum* cape blowing in the cool sea breeze, his helmet tucked beneath his arm. Imperator Octavian had placed him in command of one of nearly four hundred 109-foot long *Liburnae* ships, carrying forty-eight oarsmen and fifty soldiers heading towards the shores of Actium.

A man of medium build, Cornelius, unlike many others, did not join the army for glory, fame, or booty. He enlisted because he believed in the republic and its vision. The enemy ships loomed larger and multiplied on the horizon, with the mountain ridge of Actium Bay rising majestically behind them. In that moment, his mind fell on his family. If he were to die today, it would be in peace knowing he died bringing his family and the Republic honor. His comforting thoughts were cut short.

"General Cornelius," came a deep voice from behind.

Turning around, Cornelius came face to face with his second in command, a burly man, with both arms and chest to rival a great ape. He immediately saluted and without a prompt continued on.

"We just received a signal that Mark Anthony and Queen Cleopatra's fleet has successfully been blockaded at the mouth of Actium Bay. Imperator Octavian has given the order for a full attack," the centurion explained, before standing at attention to wait for further orders.

Cornelius exuded a sense of quiet authority as he surveyed his men diligently carrying out their duties. Inhaling deeply, he savored the crisp breeze, knowing this moment of peace was fleeting. Dropping the amethyst into a leather pouch, he strapped it onto his belt, and locked eyes with his soldier.

"Well done, lieutenant. Have the sails pulled in and the oars underway," he ordered, standing stoically at the ship's bow.

"On it, General," the soldier replied, promptly stepping back and away from his superior.

Shortly after Cornelius issued his commands, the sound of his directives echoed across the ship, carried by the bustling activity of his crew. The sailors swiftly began to retract the sails, and the rhythmic beating of the galley drum marked the beginning of their coordinated efforts. His body coiled like a spring, ready for the clash ahead. Shutting his eyes, he donned his helmet. The deck quivered beneath him as the rowers maneuvered, aligning the ship's bow to meet the enemy fleet directly.

With his eyes shut tight, Cornelius honed in on his surroundings: the brisk caress of the ocean breeze on his skin, the tang of salt intermingled with sea spray, and the steady pulse of the drum reverberating in his ears. The rhythmic drumming of the oars not only synchronized the rowers but also melded with the steady thump of his own heart, anchoring him to the present moment. With each stroke bringing them nearer to their foe, the tempo of both heart and oars quickened in unison.

Opening his eyes now focused and ready to command, they fell on the enemy's fleet of warships prowling on the distant horizon, each one flying under the banner of the legendary General Mark Anthony and Queen Cleopatra. The weight of the impending battle loomed heavy in the air. Many believed and deemed this war to be unnecessary, as Rome has already suffered one. But Cornelius believed the war to be a necessary evil, in order for Octavian to bring true peace back to the Republic.

Raising a hand into the air, behind him, Cornelius could hear the taunting of bows as arrows are nocked and pulled tautly back. The sound was promptly followed by the clanking of metal gears falling into place as six-foot ballista spears are loaded into position upon their firing carriages.

"First wave, release!" Cornelius ordered, his hand slicing the air in front of him.

A swift motion of Cornelius' hand unleashed a volley of fire arrows and ballista bolts that cut through the air, covering a distance of a hundred yards. The sky darkened as his fleet's might overshadowed the sun. The enemy ship was soon under siege, as deadly projectiles rained down on their sails, decks, and crew. In retaliation, Cornelius looked up to see a cloud of menacing weapons descending upon them from above.

"Form testudo!" bellowed Cornelius as he caught sight of the enemy's artillery barrage hurtling towards them.

Without a moment's hesitation, the soldiers swiftly converged, forming a tight formation with their scutum shields. Crafted from a blend of sturdy wood, thick leather, durable canvas, and featuring a gleaming metal umbo at its core, each shield weighed twenty-two pounds. The soldiers in the middle seamlessly interlocked their shields, while those on the flanks angled theirs to protect the sides. Together, they created an almost impenetrable barrier that encased them completely. Their movements were synchronized and exact as they banded together under their protective cover, the air vibrating with the impact of arrows striking against their shield wall.

Cornelius stood firm, his scutum shield towering at nearly forty inches in height, providing him with a steadfast barrier against the relentless barrage of metal. As the onslaught momentarily ceased, he could discern a brief respite amidst the chaos.

"Bring us to full speed," he shouted, his eyes laser focused on the enemy one hundred yards off and closing.

Cornelius's muscles tensed as he absorbed every word of his commands echoing through the ship. His fingers clenched the rail in front of him, his whole body jolting back with each synchronized push of the oarsmen on two levels, propelling the ship forward with urgency.

Thump…Thump…Thump…Thump…

The thunderous drum reverberated across the deck, commanding the attention of every soldier on board. With each powerful beat, it set their hearts racing and fueled their determination. The liburnae surged forward at seven knots, slicing through the crashing waves with precision. As the ship rode each crest, it soared briefly into the sky before plunging back down into the churning sea below.

Thump…Thump…Thump…

Seventy-five yards.

"Second wave, prepare," Cornelius continued, raising his hand into the air. He held the position for several seconds, waiting for the ship to settle back into the water to give his soldiers optimal firing sight.

Thump...Thump...Thump...

Fifty yards.

From this distance, he squinted, discerning the enemy's formation on a neighboring vessel locked in combat with their own. Intently, he zeroed in on their vulnerable broadside, oblivious to his own ship's swift and stealthy advance. Familiar with the arrangement, he recognized the precise formation his troops employed, signaling a clear intention: they were preparing for a boarding operation.

Engaging in civil strife always brought dire consequences, particularly when opposing the formidable Roman consul, Mark Anthony. Octavian was officially granted leadership of Rome's military by the Roman Senate, solidifying his position as the Republic's chosen commander, while marking Mark Anthony as a tyrant. Engaging in combat with fellow countrymen brought a bitter taste, the brutality of war leaving no room for joy. Despite the grim reality, Cornelius found resolve in the belief that by participating, he could help quell the flames of this internal conflict.

So be it! Cornelius figured. "Release!" Cornelius ordered, as the ship's bow splashed back into the blue water.

Another sharp directive from him spurred the crew into swift action, launching a fresh barrage of ballistae bolts that tore through the enemy's exposed left flank.

Thump...Thump...Thump...

Twenty-five yards.

"You've all heard what Proconsul Octavian said, 'The Republic must be unified by all means necessary.' So may our swords bring honor to the Republic, and if we fall, to our families!"

Upon catching wind of their leaders command, the crew unleashed a thunderous roar that echoed across the deck. Despite the visible signs of exhaustion etched on their faces from endless battles, Cornelius admired their unwavering loyalty to the Republic. Surrounding them, numerous enemy ships clashed in fierce combat, leaving little room for Cornelius' imposing quadriremes to strategize before launching their own attack.

Mark Anthony's quadriremes, with their bronze-plated rams gleaming under the Mediterranean sun, stood as formidable remnants of Rome's naval might. These tiered warships were a testament to the Republic's dominance at sea, striking fear into the hearts of any who dared challenge their authority on the waves.

Opting out of relying on the navy's bull, Octavian steered away from the quadriremes and instead embraced the agility of a gazelle by recruiting close to four hundred liburnae ships for the impending battle. These liburnae, previously favored by Mediterranean pirates, had undergone modifications for combat, rendering them lighter and swifter than their traditional design. With an acute understanding of each ship's vulnerabilities, Cornelius strategically navigated his vessel towards the critical midpoints, poised for tactical advantage.

"Brace!" he yelled, readying himself for the collision.

Fifteen yards.

"Brace!"

Five yards.

His iron-clad vessel surged forward like a predator hunting its prey, smashing into the midsection of the quadriremes with a deafening crash. The impact was so forceful that it tore through the enemy ships with unyielding power, slicing deep into one of them until it almost split in two. As the liburnae's ram struck their weak point above the waterline, a symphony of groans and snapping timber filled the air, sending wooden shards exploding inside the breached hull.

As the ships came to a stop, Cornelius' soldiers swiftly unleashed two corvi, each crashing down on opposite sides of the bow. The massive boarding bridge thundered down, its iron spike driving deep into the enemy's deck, locking the two ships in a fierce embrace.

While the corvi fell swiftly from the sky, it signaled Cornelius to take charge at the forefront of the gangplank. With a deft motion, he unsheathed his gladius short sword, its blade gleaming menacingly under the sun's rays. In one hand, he gripped the sword while firmly clutching his shield in the other. The Roman gladius may have been shorter compared to other swords, measuring a mere twenty-five inches from hilt to tip, but its compact design excelled in swift thrusts and precise slashes in tight combat spaces. Armed with these lethal weapons, Cornelius stood poised to lead his boarding party into action.

"Archers, release!" Cornelius ordered moments before he surged forward, to dive headlong into the heart of the fray.

On the far side, the enemy forces stood poised, their shields raised in a defensive formation while swords glinted menacingly. They moved with practiced precision, anticipation gleaming in their eyes as they awaited the impending clash.

Cornelius moved with practiced ease, his muscles reacting instinctively to the chaos around him. As he inhaled sharply, the whistling of ballistae bolts filled the air, their deadly trajectories aimed at the enemy lines. Shield-bearing foes deflected most projectiles, but a few found their mark with brutal precision. The unlucky victims, pierced through their helmets, crumpled lifelessly to the ground, swiftly replaced by fresh soldiers stepping into the fray.

Cornelius's muscles tensed as he let out a primal roar that pierced the air, signaling the start of the assault. With adrenaline coursing through their veins, his warriors surged forward behind him, storming across the gangplank with thunderous footsteps. The clash of shields reverberated as they collided with the enemy forces, setting off a chaotic and brutal skirmish on deck. Iron spears, each measuring six feet in length, whizzed through the air ahead of them. The larger ballistae projectiles effortlessly punctured the enemy's frontline, bypassing the initial soldiers as if they were mere illusions. With deadly accuracy, the bolts impaled shields and bodies, embedding themselves in the unfortunate soldiers who lingered at the rear of their ranks.

During the enemy's frantic efforts to fill the gaps in their defense, Cornelius' troops charged headlong into the fray. The clash was fierce as shields clashed, and swords met in a symphony of battle. The earlier damage caused by the ballistae gave Cornelius' soldiers an advantage, allowing them to surge forward with renewed vigor. As they stormed off the gangplank, they spread out strategically across the expansive top deck, ready to engage in close combat.

The soldiers' progress was abruptly halted when their foes swiftly encroached on their flanks, forcing a tense standoff to unfold with each side fiercely jostling for dominance.

Cornelius's jaw tightened as he planted his feet firmly on the ground, his voice cutting through the chaos like a sharp blade, "Stand strong!"

Enemy archers positioned at the rear of their ship drew back their bows, eyes narrowed in concentration as they unleashed a volley of deadly arrows. The projectiles sliced through the air with a menacing whistle, finding their marks among Cornelius' crew. Agonized screams erupted from the wounded men, mingling with the metallic clang of weapons, and the scent of blood that hung thick in the salty sea breeze. Despite the chaos unfolding around him, Cornelius remained resolute, his every command sharp and decisive. His leadership bore the unmistakable mark of battle-hardened steel, forged in the crucible of countless skirmishes and trials at sea.

With muscles straining against the weight of impending danger, the soldiers formed a protective shield, their shields locking together like an impenetrable fortress. Each warrior gritted their teeth, a sense of purpose etched into their faces, as they advanced steadily, a unified force braced for battle.

The clash of swords echoed in the air, each strike reverberating through Cornelius's shield. Time stretched thin as he stole a glance over the protective barrier, meeting the unwavering gaze of his foe. Their eyes met not with animosity but with a shared resolve born of duty. In that heartbeat of hesitation, amidst the chaos of battle, Cornelius questioned the true enemy of the Republic. As his blade clashed against those of his comrades-turned-foes, doubt crept into his mind like a shadow cast by the flickering flames of war.

The soldier's shield clattered to the ground as he stumbled, creating a gap in their defense. Cornelius seized the opportunity, his sword gleaming as it arced upwards in a swift motion. The soldier's widened eyes betrayed his realization of the grave mistake he had made in faltering, as fear and regret mingled on his face. The soldier's fate was sealed as the sword pierced his face, extinguishing any hope of seeing daylight again. With a swift and practiced movement, Cornelius withdrew his bloodied blade from the fallen enemy and seamlessly slashed through the air. The second soldier met a similar gruesome end as his head tumbled from his body, landing with a sickening thud on the ship's deck.

The force of his charge drove like a spear through the enemy ranks, cleaving their formation in two. Cornelius' warriors mirrored his assault, their swords slashing through the enemy lines with deadly precision. With the breach opened, Cornelius' troops surged forward, flooding the gap like a torrent. His strategic acumen had forced their adversaries into a desperate dilemma: face the wrath of their blades or meet a watery grave below. Victory over the ship was inevitable, its capture now only a matter of time.

In the midst of the chaos, Cornelius's soldiers charged towards the enemy, their shields raised high to deflect the incoming onslaught. The clash of metal against metal reverberated through the air as swords clashed with a deafening clang. Blood sprayed like crimson fireworks in all directions, mixing with the salty spray of seawater that sloshed onto the slippery deck, creating a gruesome mosaic of violence and sacrifice.

With a single victory nearly in his grasp, Cornelius unexpectedly began hearing, "*Brace yourself,*" being yelled through his ranks.

Cornelius's muscles tensed as a shadow loomed over him, the enemy quadrireme charging towards them. The impact was a thunderous explosion of chaos; men were hurled into the air like rag dolls, shields shattered like glass, and wooden splinters danced around them in a deadly ballet. With a sickening thud, Cornelius slammed into the unforgiving bulkhead, as darkness swallowed his vision.

I

Three Years Later

On the outskirts of Rome, a gentle breeze whispered through the air, carrying the warmth of the Mediterranean sun that bathed two swords in a dance of clashing wills. Arenius Vesta's gaze remained fixed on his opponent, each movement scrutinized with unwavering focus. A forceful push separated them momentarily before they resumed their circling, the scorching sand beneath their feet swirling in response to their duel.

Every heartbeat felt like a sledgehammer pounding against his weary muscles. The weariness seeped into his bones, threatening to drain him of strength. Losing the ability to defend himself was not an option he could entertain.

Arenius had already launched a series of attacks, each one met with a swift block or deflection, almost as if his adversary could anticipate his every move. His body was drenched in sweat and coated in a layer of dirt and sand, contrasting sharply with his opponent's pristine appearance.

Arenius accepted and understood his opponent had the upper hand in just about every category: height, size, technique, strength, and confidence. Yet there was one advantage he had over him, and this was being underestimated. He could see it in his opponent's eyes, the taunting and disapproval. Even with that, Arenius would never give in, no matter the beating. To him this was either life or death.

Grasping his sword tightly with both hands, Arenius felt rage building inside when he lunged forward with a downward slash. It was an attack his opponent was clearly expecting as he sidestepped and countered with a straight thrust at Arenius's face. Arenius watched as his opponent fell right into his trap. With precision, he baited them into a direct confrontation, knowing it would expose their vulnerable legs to his calculated strikes.

His tactic had worked. Successfully utilizing his forward motion, Arenius executed a seamless roll as the sword descended towards him, his sandals propelling a cascade of sand into the air in his wake. Coming to a halt on his knees to the immediate left of his adversary, the perfect moment to strike presented itself. A sense of triumph washed over Arenius, evident in the sly grin that crept across his face. With determination fueling his actions, he wielded his gladius with all his might. Time appeared to stretch out endlessly as the polished blade inched closer. The taste of victory lingered tantalizingly close as he prepared to deliver a decisive blow that would catch his opponent off guard.

Arenius' sword slowly inched toward his opponent's knee, and just upon contact, his opponent lifted his knee high, allowing the blow to soar cleanly beneath his foot. His opponent turned and glared deep into Arenius' eyes, it was then that Arenius was able to read their expression - *disappointment.*

To Arenius, his attack and execution was flawless. However, to the seasoned fighter facing him, this strike was nothing more than a well-rehearsed tactic easily anticipated and countered.

Sensing an opening, his opponent swiftly countered, their

blade meeting Arenius' with a resounding clash. The impact reverberated up Arenius' arm, jolting him as the sword slipped from his grasp and thudded softly onto the sandy arena floor.

Before Arenius could recover, a forceful kick crashed into his chest, propelling him backwards through the air. His body twisted in mid-air before crashing onto the ground with a heavy thud a few feet away, the wind knocked out of him as he struggled to regain his footing amidst the swirling dust.

Struggling to breathe, he desperately scoured the sandy ground for his gladius. Vulnerable and devoid of choices, Arenius sensed his heart leap into his throat with fear. The adversary stood stoically, lifting the gleaming gladius above Arenius' head. The battle had come to an end. Yet, a sense of tranquility and inevitability washed over Arenius as he acknowledged his defeat. Perhaps it was fated for him to always be on the losing side, and with a serene expression, he awaited the descending blade.

He thought of a world where he could be more, do more. A world in which he would be what he was meant to be, what others wanted him to be: *capable*. There was nothing but silence as his senses returned to him. Arenius opened his eyes to find the blade of his opponent's gladius stuck in the sand beside him. And learned he was still a part of the living world and had not yet gone on to live in the Fields of Elysium.

Meeting his opponent's gaze once more, he saw the familiar visage of his father, Cornelius, looming over him with a palpable sense of disapproval etched on his features.

"How many times have I told you? The battle is not over until your enemy is on the ground, breath no longer entering their body! It is only then that the fight is over," Cornelius yelled, extending a hand.

Arenius clasped his father's hand tightly. As he was pulled up, he noticed the firmness of his father's grip, roughened by battles fought. Even as a teenager, Arenius felt dwarfed by his father's size.

"I apologize," Arenius said, lowering his head.

Cornelius raised his son's head, "Do not be sorry. Be better," he replied, staring down at him. "If you want to survive in this world, you must perfect your technique."

Walking over he grabs Arenius' sword. Returning, "Your gladius must become an extension of you," shoving the short sword into Arenius' chest. "Knowing where it will be before your foe does. Then and only then, can you leave the fight, the victor."

"I tried," Arenius said with a whisper.

"Was that before or after smiling?" Cornelius snapped, his voice booming through the family central courtyard. Arenius stood in silence before his father.

"Cornelius, enough," Floriana interrupted as she watched from beneath the covered colonnade walkway. "Our son has surely been put through his paces today?" she said plainly. Holding a cup of water, she stepped into the sandpit, her skin glowed as an acacia tree on a mid-summers day.

"But—" Cornelius was interrupted as she gently took his head in both hands, forcing him to look at her as her brow furrowed. "Fine," he retracted, giving in to her request, taking a sip from the cup.

"Arenius, go clean yourself up," she continued. After he brushes off the sand, they both watch Arenius exit the pit.

"Son," Cornelius called out, getting Arenius to stop in his tracks. "You do know I push you because I want you to be better and stronger than I am. The Republic needs better men, better soldiers. Why not have that strength continue from our bloodline?" Arenius pounded his chest and saluted with a nod then continued to walk away. "Also help your mother prepare dinner tonight."

"Which reminds me. Arenius, I need you to ride down to the town to get a few things," Floriana cut in.

"Now?" he asked, stopping in his tracks.

"Of course, now! Besides, it will help you loosen up," Florianna added with a wink.

Frustrated, Arenius sighs and continues on.

"You sure you want to send him after what happened last time?" Cornelius retorted in a loud whisper, glancing at Arenius walking away. "Look at him."

"He will be fine. There is a reason you started training him, right? As you always say, 'Try, try, and try again.'" She whispered gently into his ear.

"You know, I will not be around this evening, and will not be back until sundown," he pleaded.

Arenius once again stopped in his tracks, facing them. Overhearing their conversation, his excitement quickly got the best of him. "Where do you have to go, Pa?"

"I have to see Augustus Caesar today. Army messenger said it was urgent," Cornelius replied hesitantly.

"Really, Augustus? May I join you?" Arenius asked with the excitement of a teenager, and the embarrassment of his defeat shoved beneath the sands he stood on.

"Not possible," Cornelius continued.

"But you always said you would take me to meet him one day. If I don't go now, there's no telling when I will have the opportunity again. Especially with him focusing on squashing rebellions in the provinces like you said."

Cornelius took a deep breath, "I'm not sure this is the right time. Besides, it will take you an hour just to go into the town for your mother, and even more time for you to clean yourself up after. I couldn't bring you before the Imperator smelling like cattle."

"I can be fast."

Floriana embraced her husband and whispered gently to him, "You did promise and how can a soldier be a soldier if he can't keep a simple promise, especially to his own son?" She pulled away then seductively walked into the house.

"Woman, I thought I married you to be on my side," he said as he watched her with keen interest as her figure subtly revealed itself beneath the flowing fabric of her tunic, tracing every contour as she moved gracefully.

"Come on, enough of that already," Arenius chimed in, receiving a blank stare from Cornelius.

"Alright. I guess it's time for you to see what your old man does."

"Yes!" he rejoiced, throwing up his hands in celebration.

"But," his father interjected, holding up his pointer finger to emphasize the matter, "hurry up."

"Of course, Papa," he chimed in eagerly, his eyes sparkling with genuine delight as he stood tall in front of him, a dimple forming on his left cheek, mirroring the wide grin that lit up his face.

"Well, get going," he ordered, waving Arenius off. *The two of them are going to have me killed*, he thought to himself.

Merely a short distance of three miles south from the Vesta residence, Trivoli stood proudly. Once an exclusive enclave for Rome's elite, it had transformed over time into a crucial resting point for travelers journeying towards Rome from the eastern lands. The town's evolution was evident in its flourishing town center, now embellished with grand temples and scholarly libraries, while bustling markets thrived on its fringes. The vigilant presence of patrolling troops ensured that under the bright midday sun, every traveler could traverse the roads without fear.

In less than an hour, Arenius arrived in town, urging his horse to pick up the pace. Despite his reluctance for completing a to-do-list, he found solace in the solitude of being away from home. The journey to Trivoli had become a routine experience - with its picturesque landscapes passing by as he traversed the lengthy roads bustling with fellow travelers. This time on the road granted him moments of introspection about his life and loved ones.

Clutching the small wax tablet containing Floriana's list of wants, he navigated through the vibrant and crowded markets. A symphony of scents enveloped him as he navigated the bustling marketplace. The air was thick with the aroma of charred meats sizzling on open flames, a medley of pungent spices from distant lands, fresh herbs crushed underfoot, and the sweet notes of aged wines lingering in wooden casks. Despite the tantalizing fragrances that tempted his senses, Arenius pressed on unwavering.

His eyes scanned the vibrant stalls adorned with colorful fabrics and gleaming trinkets, but his focus remained sharp on the task at hand. Each step he took brought him closer to his ultimate goal - to stand before the revered Augustus. As he approached the vendor that possessed the final spices Floriana requested, a prickling sensation crept up his spine.

Though no tangible presence lurked behind him when he glanced over his shoulder, a palpable sense of being shadowed lingered in the air like an unspoken threat, heightening his senses and setting his nerves on edge.

After finishing his errand, he strolled away from the bustling stall, his movements a blend of briskness and wariness. Exiting the market, he trod towards the communal stable where his horse awaited, yet the unsettling feeling of being followed lingered. Looking over his left shoulder, a chill ran down his spine as he noticed a red-headed girl trailing him twenty feet away. A glancing to the right, he saw a boy at an equal distance on the opposite side of the street, their unwavering gazes fixed solely on him.

Sensing an urgent instinct for self-preservation, he hastens his steps, deftly weaving through the bustling crowds. Glancing over his shoulder, he observes his pursuers mirroring his movements, adeptly navigating the throng and closing in on him. Faced with limited options, he propels himself into a swift sprint, hoping to outpace them and lose them in the crowd.

Noticing a wooden cart loaded with oversized clay amphorae

jars brimming with wine up ahead, Arenius swiftly approached it. He bent low beside the cart, blocking their view, then veered to the left into a cramped alleyway. He understood that he needed to shake off his pursuers entirely in order to safely return to his waiting horse. Losing his belongings and money pouch would only serve to confirm his father's doubts. This moment was crucial for him to prove his capability. Midway down the narrow alley, he stumbled upon a cluster of wooden barrels. Curiosity piqued, he glanced inside finding them empty, with survival driving him on, he cautiously stepped into one, to have his nostrils assaulted by the lingering pungency of fermenting fish sauce.

Peeking out cautiously from his hiding spot, Arenius scanned the surroundings for any sign of pursuit. The silence that enveloped the alley was eerie, devoid of any hint of human presence. Surrounded by towering barrels, he hesitated, his mind swirling with doubts about whether he was being hunted.

Did I imagine it all? Come on, Arenius, get it together, he encouraged himself.

After waiting a bit longer, he cautiously glanced towards the road. Confirming it was deserted, a chuckle escaped him for his hasty retreat. Trivoli was a bustling town after all, its size offering some reassurance that he wouldn't encounter them once more. Despite this, he knew better than to tempt fate. Emerging stealthily from the shadows of the barrels, his gaze fixated on the lively street ahead. Without hesitation, he pivoted and sprinted in the opposite direction.

With just three brisk steps, he collided forcefully with an unseen obstacle, propelling him backward onto the chilly, damp pavement. The sack of goods and the wax tablet slipped from his grasp, careening across the ground until a solitary foot intercepted their path, halting their chaotic journey.

"Look who we have here, gang," said a familiar and unfriendly voice.

Still reeling from the impact that felt like colliding with solid stone, Arenius glanced up to see three adolescents looming above him. Their parched appearances suggested a long deprivation of a bath. Lucius, slender and delicate, stood on his left, while Ava with her sprinkling of freckles was on his right. Janus, their authoritative figure, stood between them.

"What did I tell you last time, Arenius?" asked Janus, picking up the wax tablet beneath his sandal. "These are my streets, and you need my permission to market here."

"I guess that excludes the bath houses, huh?" Arenius quipped, as Ava and Lucius circled him in.

"I see our last beating didn't fix that smart tongue of yours!"

"I guess not," Arenius responded, staggering to his feet.

"What do you have for us today, momma's boy?" Janus continued, searching through the bag.

"None of your concern," Arenius snapped. As he moved closer, attempting to grab his possessions, Ava and Lucius restrained him firmly, each gripping one of his arms.

"This is not bad, Arenius. Mommy sent you with a good list this time. Tell her the list and coin pouch will make up for me wasting my time on you."

"Give it ba-"

Before Arenius could speak, Janus struck him in the stomach with a quick, forceful blow. The impact robbed him of his breath, causing him to double over in pain.

"Were you going to say, 'give it back'? Because that would be a waste of time," he smirked watching Arenius gasp air back into his lungs. "Did I hit you too hard? You would think that the son of General Cornelius could take a punch."

He lifted Arenius' head to look into his eyes. "Look at you. No wonder your father stays away from home. Who would want to be around a weak son like you?"

"You do not know of what you speak," Arenius gasped, just as two more blows doubled him over, his breath stolen by the onslaught.

Janus's attention fixed on Arenius as he passed the bag to Lucius. "Your lack of grit doesn't come from your father, it must be your feeble mother's doing. Only a fool would let their son squander coins like this," Janus remarked, his grip on Arenius's hair tightening. "Pleasure doing business with you once more," he concluded, delivering a forceful blow to Arenius's face before Lucius and Ava shoved him roughly into a murky puddle.

The world spun relentlessly around Arenius, the mocking laughter of the three attackers fading as they sauntered off with his belongings and money. Gradually, the sky sharpened into view, foretelling the inevitable disappointment awaiting him upon his return home, where his parents would once more face his empty-handed arrival.

"You'll be fine," Floriana would say, as she wiped off his dirty face, or Cornelius with his, *"Do not be sorry, be better,"* line.

Struggling to stand, a mix of blood and mud running down his face, the sting of wounds fading as thoughts of defeat consumed him. Fixing his gaze on Janus up ahead, he forced himself upright, each step fueled by others disbelief in him. Momentum building, he surged forward relentlessly until he crashed into his adversary with a primal yell that echoed through the alley. Janus barely had time to register Arenius' fierce expression before being forcefully brought to the ground.

A flurry of punches rained down swiftly: Arenius targeted

Janus's eyes, mouth, and nose with precision. Janus, caught off guard, retaliated but found each of his strikes expertly deflected by Arenius. Ava and Lucius stood frozen in terror, realizing they might be the next victims. With their leader faltering against Arenius's onslaught, they questioned their ability to intervene effectively.

"That's enough! Stop! You can have your things back," Janus pleaded, as Arenius held back the final blow.

In a sudden shift, his anger transformed into compassion as he gazed down at Janus. Fear was etched into every line of Janus's bloodied face, his eyes imploring for the torment to cease.

Locked in a tense standoff, Arenius stared directly into the eyes of Janus, his clenched fist hovering in the charged air between them. In that heartbeat of connection, a flicker of realization crossed Arenius' face - a sudden understanding dawned upon him. Janus, the tormentor, was merely navigating the hand he had been dealt in life.

"What's going on down there?" shouted a woman passing the alley.

While Arenius was preoccupied, Lucius swiftly nudged him away from his companion, assisted Janus to his feet, and with Ava the three hastily spirited away, abandoning the forgotten wax tablet, jingling coins, and bundled belongings. Sitting on the ground, Arenius remained frozen in place as the trio bolted into the distance along the bustling main thoroughfare.

"Are you alright my boy?" the woman asked, waiting for a reply.

Sitting on the ground and taking in his blood-soaked knuckles, Arenius failed to acknowledge the woman, who promptly waved him off and continued on her way. Coming back to his own, he took note of the sun's position in the sky and immediately snatched the items off the ground and ran.

"How am I going to explain this?" Arenius pondered, his muscles straining with each determined push.

The Vesta villa nestled amidst the serene countryside, a peaceful retreat located a few miles away from the bustling town of Trivoli, to the east of majestic Rome. The grand domus was divided into two distinct square sections: the primary section, boasting a second floor, housed the heart of the home with its vibrant kitchen, inviting dining area, and welcoming social spaces. Meanwhile, the secondary section was dedicated solely to luxurious sleeping quarters where tranquility reigned supreme. The air around the villa danced with the enchanting scent of Lavender, carried by gentle breezes from the undulating hills adorned with endless rows of this fragrant herb, enveloping all who ventured there in a calming embrace.

Their dwelling, embodied Cornelius and Floriana's dream retirement abode, a sanctuary far removed from the bustling streets of Rome. Through numerous military exploits, plundered treasures, and his promotion to the prestigious rank of tribune following the triumph at Actium, Cornelius had amassed sufficient wealth to secure both land and this charming residence for Floriana. Escaping the squalid Roman alleys had always topped his list of priorities. Unlike most aristocrats who relied on servants and slaves, Cornelius considered himself superior even to those seated in the Senate, advocating for his family to earn their keep through honest toil.

"Come on, we have no time for this," Cornelius urged. Dressed in his best armor, he continued to prepare both horses with their saddles to travel into the city.

In the home's vestibule, Floriana ensures Arenius' presentation is flawless by adjusting his white and blue tunic before going in front of Rome's greatest leader.

"Not to worry, Rome will be there, it has been for hundreds of years," Floriana said with a hint of amusement, causing Cornelius to throw up his hands in defeat. Giving her attention back to Arenius, she gently caressed the shiner forming beneath his eye.

"I will be fine," Arenius insisted, turning his face away.

"Arenius, I want you to have this as you go before Augustus."

"I do not need anything, Ma," he protested, gently pulling away to leave. "You know Pa is going to blame me if we are late."

Holding him in place, "Your father doesn't see you that way," she said, doing her best ease his tension.

"I sure can't tell," he murmured, his gaze locked onto his father a short distance away."

"That's beside the point, anyway this will bring you good fortune," Floriana continued, taking out a leather pouch, she emptied its contents into his hands.

"What is it?" Arenius asked as the small uncut purple stone necklace fell into his hand. The stone, with its jagged edges and unpolished surface, captivated him in a way no other rock had before. Its raw beauty was unparalleled.

"It's an amethyst stone," she said.

"This is amazing, where did you get it?"

"Well, your father is actually the one who got it for you while he was campaigning in Egypt before the Battle of Actium."

"Why was he not the one to give it to me?" Arenius turned to fix his gaze on Cornelius again, who was doing his best to remain patient.

II

"You know how your father is. He may not be the most affectionate person; he is a soldier after all. But underneath that armor, he is as tender as Cupid and loves you dearly."

"Enough talk, let's go," Cornelius cut in, seeing Floriana pampering Arenius.

Floriana responded with a glare which meant only one thing, *WHEN I AM DONE.* Knowing this was one battle he would not win, he went back to the horses.

Giving her attention back to Arenius, "He told me he was looking for the right time, and I believe now is the time," she doted, looking into his eyes. "Turn around and let me put it on you."

As the stone was fastened securely around Arenius' neck, a peculiar sensation coursed through him, unlike anything he had ever experienced. It felt akin to a gentle murmur carried on a tranquil breeze, as if a weight had been effortlessly lifted from his very being.

"There now, let me look at you," she said, turning him back around. "Something wrong?" she asked, seeing the confusion upon his face.

"*Ahh*, no Ma. Just taking in the stone," he reported uneventfully, brushing off the feeling.

"Arenius, let's go! I can't keep Caesar waiting."

Floriana snaps to Cornelius, "I'm sure Augustus Caesar, or whatever new title the would-be holy senate has given Octavian, is capable of keeping himself busy until you arrive."

"Watch your mouth, my love. You know what would happen if someone heard you talking like that?"

"I assume, be thrown to the lions, life in prison. Good thing we own a house with no one else around besides us," Floriana smiled, going back to Arenius. "Ok, my young general. Go before your father's impatience causes the mountains to fall," she finished, kissing Arenius on the forehead. "May Mercury light your path."

"Love you, too," Arenius said, giving a soft smile before running to join Cornelius who had already exited the home.

Floriana followed them out the door and watched them mount their horses.

"Bring our son back in one piece," she demanded, leaning against the foyer's colonnade.

"What about me?" Cornelius asked playfully.

"And Arenius, keep your father out of trouble. The big city tends to bring out the worst in him," she added with the same playful smile.

"I'll do my best," Arenius replied, conscious of Cornelius' intense gaze fixed on him. Pushing aside the prickling feeling, he nudged his horse forward with a click of his heels, guiding it towards the winding road ahead.

"We will return as soon as we can. I love you," Cornelius ended, pulling on the horse's harness, guiding it down the dirt path.

III

The pathways leading to Rome, the Eternal City, teemed with a diverse array of travelers hailing from distant lands. They carried a myriad of commodities destined for every corner of the vast Roman Empire. Following Octavian's ascension to Augustus, the Republic underwent numerous transformations, resulting in an unprecedented economic prosperity that had eluded it for ages. As a result of his leadership, Rome emerged as a shining example to nations far and wide.

Approaching the towering Esquiline Gate from the east, Arenius took note of the vibrant blend of locals and foreigners mingling in the crowd. This ancient arch, one of Rome's many stone gateways that had stood guard over the city for ages, held a sense of history and protection.

Unlike Cornelius, a seasoned general who had traversed these gates numerous times in service to Rome, Arenius was a stranger to such urban journeys, having mostly stayed close to their villa. Yet, through his father's dedication to the Republic, Arenius felt a deep bond with the city and its noble traditions.

Nevertheless, despite the obstacles, Arenius couldn't help but feel a sense of wonder as he observed the diverse array of travelers passing through the newly renovated white stone gate. Whether they were transporting goods on carts, riding majestic horses, or strolling leisurely, each figure added to the vibrant tapestry of Rome's bustling entrance. The sight of Rome's magnificence unfolding before his eyes filled Arenius with a profound sense of belonging to a greater whole. In that moment, he realized that he was not just an individual but an integral part of a city that radiated illumination to the entire world.

Leading the way, Cornelius guided their horses towards a quaint stable located just beyond the Esquiline Gate. A diligent stable hand, accustomed to attending to soldiers' steeds, hastened over to assist them with their mounts. Once their horses were safely taken care of, Arenius and Cornelius made their way towards the imposing gates of the city.

Despite being the most formidable authority in the known world, Rome stood vigilant, with a pair of soldiers stationed on each side of the entrance. As Cornelius strode through, both soldiers immediately identified their tribune and respectfully saluted him as he passed by.

Strolling beneath the colossal stone archway, Arenius found himself pondering why Cornelius had never shown him this city during their time living just a half day's journey away. His curiosity ebbed away as he marveled at the grandeur of the gate, its towering height reaching over forty feet above him.

"I see your mother gave you the necklace." Cornelius commented, taking in Arenius' bruised face, while he was too distracted with taking in their nation's legacy.

"Yes, she did. Thank you," Arenius responded, clutching the necklace then averted his eyes to focus on the paved road ahead.

"I told her to wait. But who am I to get your mother to heed a man's word? That Spartan blood of hers," shaking his head. "And now you share that same blood as hers. Anyhow, I was told it brings strength to the wearer," Cornelius said, eyeing the stone around his sons neck.

"I believe it, I feel different already," Arenius said excitedly.

"Calm down, Arenius. I am sure it is just a stone. Nice looking but still a stone. Vendor most likely fabricated the story for the superstitious folk. Besides, true virtue and strength comes from the heart. Forged by one's own hand, you understand?"

"Yes, sir," Arenius replied, locking his eyes ahead of them.

For a brief spell, they strolled side by side, enveloped in the clamor of hawkers hawking their wares and the rattle of wooden carts passing by.

Observing the faint downturn of Arenius' lips after his final statement, Cornelius decided to speak up, eager to dispel the somber atmosphere. "We arrived a bit earlier than expected. So, let us take a quick trip through the Forum before heading for the House of Augustus."

Arenius inclined his head quietly, a faint smile tugging at the corners of his lips as a glimmer of light entered his eyes.

Dubbed the Eternal City, Rome presented a labyrinthine challenge for all but its most devoted inhabitants who had mastered its intricate layout. This unplanned metropolis sprawled across seven hills, each hill riddled with serpentine alleys and cramped pathways. Each of these hills served a unique purpose within the city, with the prominent Capitoline Hill standing as the revered site of the temple dedicated to Jupiter Optimus Maximus. Nestled at the foot of this temple resided the Roman Forum, pulsating at the core of the bustling city.

As he walked along the Via Sacra, Rome's hallowed thoroughfare, Arenius took in the living tapestry of Roman society in all its authenticity. Venturing into the Roman Forum, he encountered a bustling scene filled with vibrant energy. The air was thick with the scent of incense as individuals engaged in rituals to honor the gods, while others gathered to listen attentively to speeches delivered by up-and-coming political figures.

Towering structures surrounded them in the bustling forum, some soaring to heights that left Arenius in awe. Among them stood the grandest of all, the Basilica Aemilia, a colossal edifice stretching three hundred and twenty-eight feet in length and ninety-eight feet in width. Its three tiers gleamed with African marble, radiating a majestic aura akin to Mount Olympus basking in the warm embrace of the setting sun.

"By the gods, look at that," Arenius said with astonishment, taking in the massive structure. "Have you ever been inside?"

"Of course, but I prefer when my duties keep me away like today."

"Can we go in?"

"Not now, we really have to move along. Believe me when I say, You're not missing much. The outside maybe pretty, but inside, its hot and full of insane people yelling at each other in court," Cornelius added with a faint smile, patting Arenius on the shoulder before leading him away.

Navigating the winding path to the House of Augustus perched on the Palatine Hill proved to be a challenging journey, necessitating frequent halts at various security posts, particularly cumbersome for Cornelius weighed down by his complete suit of armor.

"Never gets easier," Cornelius said as he breathed deeply upon reaching the top of the long winding ramp. "Must be the armor. Look at you, not one bead of sweat on your head."

"Must be my excitement of finally seeing the city," Arenius

replied while taking in the view of the city from upon the hill. "Thank you, Pa, for bringing me. You can see for miles from here."

"It is my duty to show you the glory of the Republic," he said, resting a firm hand on his son's shoulder. "If you work hard, maybe one day you can leave your mark on its long legacy."

"Excuse me, Tribune Vesta," interrupted a soldier, unlike any other soldiers Arenius had ever seen, this one was wearing an armor as dark as obsidian. "Augustus Caesar has been waiting for you. Please come with me." Without waiting for a response, the soldier made a quick about face, and started to walk off.

Cornelius paused, silent and still, as though caught in a trance. Arenius watched him closely, wondering if the soldier's armor had unsettled Cornelius just as it had unsettled him.

"Pa, is everything alright, " Arenius asked.

"Of course," Cornelius nodded, his focus returning. "All is in order. We'll table our discussion about Rome for now," he reassured Arenius with a series of friendly pats on the shoulder as he followed behind the soldier.

Arenius lingered for a brief moment, committing the view of the city to memory before following behind his father's footsteps.

The opulence of the House of Augustus left any visitor in awe. Intricate statues of gods adorned the halls, while vivid frescoes depicted lush landscapes and exotic wildlife. The rhythmic sound of their footsteps echoed on the mosaic floor as they followed their guide through sheltered walkways, finally entering a majestic atrium supported by towering columns painted in regal shades of purple.

"Wait here," ordered the soldier after stepping a few feet into the atrium. Leaving them their guard escort made his way toward a group of men having a discussion on the other side of the atrium.

"Is that him?" asked Arenius, pointing to the group.

"Yes, that's Augustus Caesar wearing the gold trimmed toga. And don't point," Cornelius said, with a whispered command.

"What of the others?" Arenius asked curiously.

"The other two in broad purple striped *tunicas* are senators; which senators, I have not a clue," Cornelius answered, keeping his gaze on the group of men. "And if you have no more questions, stay quiet. And do not speak unless asked to."

Peering from afar, Arenius was taken aback by the sight of Augustus. Contrary to his imagination, Augustus did not possess the imposing figure he had anticipated – a towering giant with a commanding presence akin to his father's. Despite the legendary stories circulating about Augustus' victorious battles, Arenius had envisioned him as a formidable warrior above all else.

Instead, he saw a man of youthful demeanor, average in stature, with skin as pale as winter snow, hinting at a life shielded from the sun's touch. His hair gleamed like spun gold and his slender frame stood in stark contrast to the typical image of Rome's military leader. Despite his unassuming appearance, Arenius sensed an undeniable aura of authority emanating from him - a potent force that could send shivers down one's spine merely by being near it.

To Arenius it felt like minutes had passed before their guide finally reached Augustus and saluted him. After a few exchanges of words from Augustus the two senators dismissed themselves as the guard began to debrief his leading commander.

"*Ah*, Tribune Cornelius, hero of Actium," Augustus greeted, his youthful sounding echoing off the large rooms walls as he waves them over.

"Remember not to say a word unless spoken to," Cornelius repeated with a whisper, his gaze locked on Augustus making his way toward them. "Augustus Caesar," Cornelius saluted.

"No formal greetings needed," Augustus said.

"Sorry about my lateness. My son has never been to our great city and now that he's of age, I thought it would do him some good to know what the Republic offers the world."

"How wise of you, general. The Republic does offer much to this chaotic world we live in. Yet with Rome being a beacon of light, there will be peace throughout her territories," Augustus assured him. "Now for you, son of a great tribune, what do you think of our beloved Republic?"

Arenius remained silent and glanced at Cornelius, who stood proud and strong for guidance.

"Sorry, Augustus, he's not aware of our formalities," Cornelius apologized, cutting an eye at Arenius who glanced away. "Arenius, answer!"

"He is fine, may just need time to adjust," Augustus assured, smiling at Arenius.

Breathing in deeply, "I find her most beautiful, a gift to the world," Arenius replied.

"Do you, now? And how do you plan to aid the Republic with spreading its light?" Augustus asked, a genuine smile dawning on his face.

Arenius took a moment in silence to think on the question, then responded, "By becoming a mightier soldier than my father, he has trained me in military strategy and combat."

"Well. I could not expect a better answer than that, can I, Tribune Vesta?" he said, adjusting his toga. "With that being said, I hope you made them regret their mistakes." He pointed to the boy's bruised eye.

"That's a mark from our time in the training pit together," Cornelius chimed in again. "But he's smart and works hard. Given time I believe he will become what Rome needs," Cornelius continued, nodding at Arenius. "Augustus, you summoned me, and I do not want to waste more of your time discussing the boy."

Pausing to think and staring at Arenius, "You are right, the Senate does wish for my presence today. Just continue to keep this young soldier working hard."

"I will," Cornelius affirmed, nodding resolutely as Augustus took his leave. "Arenius, hold your place on the bench," he instructed without breaking his stride.

Following the directions given, Arenius made his way to the marble bench and settled down, a mix of unease and determination churning within him. Despite being in the presence of Augustus Caesar, he couldn't shake the feeling that Cornelius doubted his worth.

"When is hard work going to mean something? When is anything ever good enough for you?" Arenius questioned while sitting there tightly clutching the carved marble bench when suddenly the amethyst stone around his neck began to pulse with light.

Worried about attracting attention, he cradled the stone in his palms, trying to conceal its glow. As soon as he shielded the stone, its pulsing intensified, and suddenly, he was thrust out of his physical form. From this new perspective, he observed his motionless body on the bench below, trapped in a momentary pause along with those in the room.

"What is this?" Arenius exclaimed, his words reverberating *through the ethereal realm. Despite his presence in this unfamiliar astral plane, he maintained a peculiar connection that allowed him*

to perceive glimpses of the tangible world beyond.

There was a veil dividing the two worlds. His world, the world he was familiar with, was present but only as a projection of some sort. Though the world he now found himself in was empty, he felt at peace, and weirdly sure of himself.

In a blink, he found himself transported to a bustling marketplace. The air was thick with the clang of metal against metal and the shouts of vendors hawking their wares. Amidst the chaos, he stood transformed into a warrior, his muscles taut with anticipation. Across the square, a colossal wooden horse loomed large, its construction a testament to impending war. And then... the world around him blurred as if caught in a whirlwind.

Zipping through space once more, he found himself in a grand tent filled with opulent tapestries. From the perspective of a woman, he crept towards a slumbering figure sprawled on the lush carpet. Silently, she positioned a gleaming tent peg against his temple and hoisted her mallet. With precision, she struck the peg, propelling him into another realm. This cycle repeated itself relentlessly. Each time he inhabited a new existence, experiencing diverse lives as different individuals, forging profound connections with each before abruptly returning to his own body.

Upon opening his eyes, Arenius experienced a surge in his senses: the melodic chirping of birds outside, the rhythmic sound of slaves moving around. It felt like a hidden aspect of himself had been illuminated, akin to a candle being lit within him.

As the glow from the necklace dimmed, he discerned a chorus of voices emanating from his father's vicinity. With an inexplicable clarity, he zeroed in on Cornelius and Augustus engaged in conversation.

"Ever since you helped squash Mark and Cleopatra's rebellion, the people of Rome have really taken to you," Augustus shared.

Fascinated by his newfound powers, Arenius watched Augustus speaking with his father, his attention drawn to the ethereal tentacles slowly unfurling from Augustus' back. Blinking in disbelief, he saw one appear, then another, until a multitude of sinuous tendrils danced in and out of sight like spectral ribbons. The atmosphere grew dense and oppressive, carrying a faint hint of sulfur on its breath. Expecting a reaction from Cornelius to this strange occurrence, Arenius was met with only silence.

Arenius couldn't comprehend how the anomaly had eluded his father, who stood side by side with it. He vigorously rubbed his eyes before fixing his gaze on Augustus once more, only to discover that the mysterious occurrence persisted.

Augustus' gaze transfixed, the entity oozed from his back, merging to create a monstrous form that sent shivers down Arenius' spine. The smoke twisted into a beast, manifesting its upper body as it slithered out of Augustus. This creature bore resemblance to a bear, its crimson fur more vivid than blood-soaked earth, its claws and fangs deadlier than any weapon forged in Rome. Along its spine, jagged horns gleamed like cursed jewels, exuding an aura of impending doom.

Cornelius and Augustus conversed quietly beneath the looming creature when, out of nowhere, the monstrous being swiveled its head towards Arenius. Their gazes locked in a chilling moment that seemed to convey a silent message of 'I ACKNOWLEDGE YOU.' Arenius squirmed uneasily in his chair, but to his own amazement, he held his ground, silently willing the creature to vanish from his sight. Just as swiftly as it had materialized, the swirling smoke started to thin out and gradually receded back into the confines of Augustus' back.

"I would not know, Caesar, too much time in the countryside

I guess," Cornelius replied.

Augustus laughed, "Well, I'm telling you; the people love you. So, with the people's recognition, I would like you to command the Praetorians."

"Praetorians?" Cornelius questioned.

"Yes, my soon to be private guard. You have to had noticed the soldier that escorted you in, they are just one of many to come."

"I observed the intricate design of the armor, assuming it was crafted for ceremonial purposes. To celebrate your many accomplishments, Caesar," Cornelius remarked casually.

Augustus laughed, "No ceremony here my friend, just a precaution. With all the civil unrest from the past years, I plan to enlist amazing soldiers like yourself, to keep, let us say, the unfaithful from reaching me. The same could not been said for my father," He pointed towards a vibrant deified statue of Julius Caesar, its colors striking against the backdrop. "Anyways, you and your family will be compensated, and I will make sure you receive a worthy estate of your choosing here in Rome, with pay. What do you say?" he asked, placing a firm hand on Cornelius' shoulder.

"May I speak freely, Augustus?" Cornelius asked respectfully.

Despite a subtle shift in his stance, Augustus kept his serene expression intact. "Of course, General. You are not just a key commander to me; you are a trusted ally," Augustus assured, gently letting go of Cornelius' shoulder.

"Well, Caesar, I was hoping that after my term I would be able to settle in one of the provinces and live out my days in peace with my family."

"Family is important, believe me I know," he confirmed, placing both hands his back and staring Cornelius in his eyes, "but would you also agree the Republic is more important? A

Republic we have been fighting for, for years. When the great Caesar, went on to become a god," as Augustus talk he led him over to the nearby life size statue of Julius Caesar, wearing a purple toga and golden laurel upon his head, "he blessed and entrusted me to continue in his work of keeping Rome great. Doing all that is necessary for our Republic. This position is not simply for me, you'll be taking it for Rome." He faced Cornelius to look more deeply into his eyes. "I will allow you to think about it some more. I know it is a big decision."

"My Lord," Cornelius said, drawing his right fist to his left should in a slight bow of agreement.

"Let's leave it at that," Augustus interjected, raising a hand to hush him. "Go on, take your son and relish the splendor of this day. You have my permission to explore every corner of my estate. Let him witness firsthand the fruits of your labor."

"Caesar," Cornelius saluted and excused himself, knowing his freedom of speech was up and trying to convince Augustus otherwise would only be futile.

Cornelius stood in the grand hall, his meeting with Augustus unfolding in a way he could never have foreseen. Anticipating accolades to secure a brighter future for his family, he found himself faced with an unexpected twist - an offer of another term of service. Years dedicated to Rome now stretched ahead indefinitely, disrupting the retirement plans he had meticulously crafted. The weight of Caesar's request bore down on him, contrary to his every intention.

From his position Arenius watched as Augustus' guard approached his leader's side and the two of them watched Cornelius' departure. Arenius began to hear something odd, like the mixture of flowing water and wind. Focusing his senses, what was once inaudible turned into murmuring and seemed to be emanating from Augustus and the guard.

"Is that talking? Can't be, their lips aren't moving," Arenius thought.

He kept his attention locked on them, as their eyes were locked on his father. He could not make out all that was being said, for what he was hearing was mixed with hisses and unworldly growls. He struggled to make out the words as his senses were being combated against, purposely keeping their words at bay.

"Let's go, Arenius," Cornelius commanded as he caught up to him, his long cape billowing behind him as he strode ahead without missing a step.

Arenius follow suit behind his father when the hissing formed into words, *"Make sure...If not persuaded...end him!"* His eyes went wide as he locked eyes with Augustus until he completely turned the corner.

Soft wisps of clouds drifted lazily across the dusky sky, painting a warm orange glow over the undulating hills of the countryside as the sun dipped towards the horizon. Arenius and Cornelius rode in silence, their steeds steadily carrying them away from Rome and the imposing House of Augustus where tensions had simmered just an hour before.

Arenius recognized the familiar grim expression on his father's face, a sign of his deep-seated frustration at being trapped in a situation beyond his control. In such moments, Arenius usually his father to be or awaited Floriana's intervention to resolve the brewing conflict.

Having little traffic on the late evening roads and no guards within earshot, there was no better time than to ask for an explanation for what he had seen before they reach home. As their horses' hooves echoed against the cobblestones, Arenius prepared to speak.

"Pa, can I tell you something?"

"Not now, Arenius," he replied without hesitation, while maintaining his focus on the road.

"It is about today."

"I said not now!"

"It is important and if not now, then when?" Arenius blurted.

Pulling on the reins, Cornelius stopped his horse in its tracks to face his son. "What part of not now, do you not understand? I suppose it is the part, when you will not let me think about how to tell your mother we have to stay in Italy because I am not allowed to say no to my commander. Is this what you want to talk about? Or did those kids in Trivoli also knock your head too hard for you to understand?"

Arenius watched his father's outburst with a calm detachment that surprised even himself. The usual sting of his father's harsh words seemed to have lost its edge, replaced by a sense of understanding that he couldn't quite explain. It was almost as if the stone had somehow altered his perception, leaving him feeling strangely transformed ever since that peculiar encounter.

After a moment of silence, "What? I figured you would simply turn down further offers to remain in the army."

"What? How do you-," Cornelius sighs and gathers himself seeing disappointment across Arenius' face. "Never mind. It is nothing you need to concern yourself with, son."

"I am sorry Pa, I know how much retiring meant to you."

"Stop right there! I do not need any pity! If we have to stay to honor Rome, then we stay."

"Do you actually believe that?"

"What did you say?" Maneuvering the horse parallel to Arenius' horse, to be face to face. "This time you better choose your words carefully. Your mother may let you get away with it, but I dare you to curse the blood split for the Republic in my face."

Arenius took a deep breath, "I said do you believe that? Because Augustus does not."

Cornelius raised his hand menacingly towards his son, poised to bring him down from his horse. However, instead of cowering in fear, Arenius stood firm, meeting his father's gaze unwaveringly.

Sensing something different in his son, he lowered his hand, "You could be imprisoned for these words. Do you want that? Do you want to bring dishonor to your mother and I?"

"No! All I do is for our family. But what I saw today, was beyond you or our family."

"What are you talking about? The journey must be going to your head in order for you to believe you comprehended anything you saw today."

"Not that," Arenius corrected.

"Then what are you going on about," Cornelius said dismissively.

"Today, when you were talking to Augustus, I saw...I saw..."

"You saw what? The commander and leader of the Republic give orders to one of his subordinates, that is it. Well, that is how this all works; he gives orders, I obey! Clearly this is something you have not mastered yet!"

"Why are you always so critical of me? I only seek your validation, even though it always seems out of reach!" Arenius exclaimed, trying to steady his racing heart with slow, deliberate breaths.

"Honor and loyalty is not given, even to children. It is earned by one's lifestyle and on the battlefield."

"I'm not amidst a battlefield," Arenius yelled, halting his father's words momentarily. "Moreover, what I witnessed today was beyond our kind—a creature of unknown origins," Arenius elucidated.

"Now you are not making sense."

"I saw a grotesque bear come out of Augustus Caesar's back, burning with smoke. It looked right at me as though it knew me. And with its scowl, I have no doubt that it meant me harm."

"I saw no such thing. This is nonsense and nothing but the imagination of a boy," Cornelius protested, getting his horse back underway.

"I know, I was there when you kept talking to him. But that does not mean it did not happen," Arenius continued, riding his horse beside him to keep pace.

"I do not want to hear any more of this delusion. And if you do not want to be view as being mad, I suggest for you not mention it to anyone. I do not want our family put in chains for your childish imagination."

"It was not an imagination!"

"I said, I do not want to hear about it. I have enough to think about. I knew it was a bad idea to bring you. I should have left you home with your mother where you belong," Cornelius finished, his words trailing off with the evening wind.

Arenius eased his horse to a gentle halt, fixing his gaze on his father who rode ahead. Despite his father's esteemed status as a general and his deep reverence for honor, Arenius couldn't ignore the lingering sense that Cornelius had never truly embraced the essence of fatherhood.

"Come on, boy. The last thing I want to tell your mother is that you were stolen by thieves in the night."

IV

Two hours had passed, and now they found themselves back in the comfort of their cozy home. Arenius rolled up his sleeves and began assisting with the preparations for the family dinner.

"Can you set out the dates, Arenius? My hands are occupied at the moment." Floriana asked as she cooked food on the kitchen grill, a bed of flaming charcoal burning beneath in a specially made trough.

Arenius grabbed bowls and spoons from the counter across the room, when Cornelius slid behind his wife and peeked over her shoulder. Witnessing the scene unfolding, Arenius shook his head and exited the kitchen.

"How about a taste?" Cornelius asked, gently kissing her on the ear and neck.

"No samples." Floriana quipped.

"Who said I was speaking only of food?"

"Like I said, no samples," she said playfully smiling.

"It has been a long day. Just a taste would make things a whole lot better," he whispered in her ear.

"We eat together or not at all," she continued, using a wooden spoon to stir a small iron pot of bean and carrot soup.

Next to the soup were strips of roasted venison. Pears roasted next to the venison. And next to the pears, a few oysters were nearly done, as the shells were beginning to open.

"Now go lie down," Floriana said, swiftly slapped Cornelius' hands with the wooden spoon as they crept around her waist, prompting him to retract them hastily.

"You do know I am the man of the house, right?" he playfully chuckled, flicking his hand as if shooing away a pesky fly, dispelling the lingering ache from the strike.

"Well in this kitchen, I am lord," she smiled.

Understanding the nuances of failure, Cornelius plants a gentle kiss on her cheek before leaving the kitchen. As he enters the dining room, he spots Arenius reclining on one of the three klinai couches encircling a lavish spread of food. The delicacies are elevated off the ground, inviting them to relax in opulence while indulging in their meal.

Cornelius, relieved to be free of his heavy armor, strolled into the dining chamber. Silently, he reclined on his klinai, plucked a couple of ripe grapes from a nearby bowl, and savored their sweetness. The soft glow of bronze oil lamps placed strategically in the room heightened the palpable tension hanging in the air, accentuating the unspoken communication between him and Arenius.

Arenius sat apart, his gaze briefly meeting Cornelius's before he sank into the plush couch. The silence thickened like a fog, creating a chasm akin to the expanse between rival realms. Just as the oppressive stillness threatened to engulf them, Floriana arrived bearing bowls brimming with the last of the savory roasted delicacies, setting them down on the polished table.

"The journey must have been something for neither of you not to be eating," she stated resting out on her side.

"We were waiting for you. I heard you wanted to eat as a family," Arenius added, cutting another eye to his father, who remained quiet.

"I am here, so enjoy," Floriana said, giving her motherly smile, that seemed to add some much-needed light to the room.

The flickering light from the lamps cast shifting shadows across the room as the trio dined without exchanging a word. Soon, the table was nearly empty, save for a partially consumed loaf of bread and a small bowl containing just a handful of venison strips.

"How was the visit with Augustus?" Floriana asked, breaking the silence.

"It went well," Cornelius responded, chewing on a piece of meat.

"As well as seeing demons could be," Arenius whispered.

"I said enough of that!" Cornelius growled, giving Arenius a death glare.

"Cornelius! No yelling at dinner, my dear," her words trailing into the night. "Please, tell me how was Rome," she continued, smiling politely, eyes locked on her husband.

"Augustus asked me to join his personal guard," he replied, his voice low.

"And you are now just mentioning this? I know my cooking is good, but it is not that good. What did you say? You did not agree, did you? We already made plans to relocate after your term," Floriana questioned, setting her plate aside to give him her full attention.

"No, I did not agree," taking a deep breath, "I told him I will have an answer by tomorrow," Cornelius continued, taking a grape and eating it.

"Your answer is going to be no, correct?" Floriana asked, her eyes locked on him.

"I do not know what my answer is going to be!"

"But I can't imagine Augustus accepting, 'no', as an answer. Why you withhold this?" She continued.

"How was I supposed to tell you, when I just learned about it? I am looking, well, was looking forward to the end of my term. Do you think I have had enough?" Cornelius said, his voice elevated slightly.

"Of course, I do. And like you, we were also looking forward to it. You have spent more year's campaigning than at home with your family. I can handle it, but Arenius needs you," her eyes falling on Arenius, who was clearly not expecting those words.

"Rome needed me and I went! There is no us, no food, or villa without Rome! You understand?" Cornelius's frustration erupted as he slammed his fist onto the table, sending objects tumbling and scattering across the surface.

They froze in place, their hearts racing, trying to make sense of the sudden turn of events when a series of sharp knocks echoed through the room. Their gazes locked, silently questioning each other, *"Do you know who that could be?"* The knocking continued, growing more urgent with each rap on the door.

"Remain seated, your efforts suffice," Cornelius commanded, halting Arenius as he began to stand from the plush couch. With a dignified posture, Cornelius took his leave and made his way towards the vestibule. However, just before exiting, he paused at the entrance of the dining room. Without looking back at them, "Besides, living in Rome could be exactly what the boy needs," he said, walking off before Floriana could respond.

Reaching the door, Cornelius glanced at his gladius hanging on a hook near the door. Living on quiet farm lands far from Rome, made having guests even far unlikely, making having his weapon near a must, in order to be prepared for the unexpected. With a twist of the handle, their door creaked open for him to find two of Augustus' Praetorian guards standing their black armor gleaming in the light of the full moon.

Cornelius failed to recognize either of the soldiers, so he promptly committed them to memory. One of the soldiers' age was starting to show with a mixture of gray and brown hairs sprouting from beneath his helmet, most likely a career soldier. The other was a young man, no older than twenty-two, about 5'9 and having muscles to rival Cornelius'.

"Can I help you?" Cornelius greeted, scanning the area behind them for any additional soldiers, only to see their two horses standing quietly hitched to a tree.

"Sorry to bother you at this time, Tribune," the older soldier replied, both saluting in the process. "We have a word from Caesar. May we come in?"

Cornelius eyed both men down, finding nothing out of place but them being there, "Sure, you may enter," Cornelius said, stepping back, he allowed both men inside.

Before shutting the door he scanned the grounds in front their home. He found outside as it has always been with fireflies dancing in the dark beneath a high full moon. The only sounds were that of the soldiers snorting horses hitch against a tree. Feeling at ease he closed the door shut.

"What is this about soldiers?" Cornelius continued, turning to face the soldiers.

"Tribune Vesta, Augustus Caesar requires your expertise on a matter in Rome," responded the older soldier. Though speaking normally, his raspy voice carried within their home.

"No problem, soldier. Please let Caesar know I will be there before day break," reaching for the door's handle he attempted to dismiss his guests.

"Sorry, there is a misunderstanding," the older Praetorian

said, reaching out, preventing Cornelius from fully opening the door.

"Caesar wants to see you now. We have orders to escort you to the meeting location," the young soldier chimed in.

"Now?" Cornelius questioned, staring the young man in his eyes.

"Yes, now. And we should not linger and keep Caesar waiting," the young Praetorian insisted.

For an instant, as his gaze met the young soldier's, something flickered in Cornelius's eyes—something he saw, or perhaps remembered. Not the look of an eager soldier trying to find his place amongst their ranks. No, it was something he had not seen in some time; hate, pure wrath and rage, the sort of anger someone has for someone who had taken the soul of a loved one.

"Ok," Cornelius agreed, cautiously allowing the door to settle back, releasing the handle.

"What's happening, Cornelius? Is everything all right?" Floriana asked entering the vestibule and seeing the soldiers. The soldier's attention promptly went to Arenius standing by her side, who quickly gained the attention of the older soldier.

"All is well, my love. You and Arenius have my leave to return to dinner. When finished I want you to head to your mother's. I have business with Augustus, and I may be gone a few days," Cornelius responded, eyes still locked with the young soldier's. No one moved as an eerie silence encapsulated the foyer. "Go now, Floriana." Seeing his family exit, he faced the praetorians. "Ok, give me a moment to grab my things," he said, taking a few steps back into the house.

"No need, general," the young soldier hissed, stepping forward and grabbing hold of his sword's handle.

Cornelius took in the gesture, his mind immediately repeating what Arenius had spoken. Not mythical demons or parallel plans, but how Augustus seemed off, and not himself. This was no private escort, they were here for an assassination. Simply for hesitating, or worse, refusing Augustus' proposal.

"I am a Tribune. And I don't leave my house without my armor, let alone enter Rome. Being Caesar's guards, you should know the dishonor in that," Cornelius reassured, standing with confidence.

"Sorry. Orders from Caesar are to bring you and your son back. Without delay," insisted the older soldier.

"My son, why my son," he questioned.

"Forgive my forwardness, but you know how this works, Tribune. We're given orders and we don't ask questions," the older Praetorian said, remaining stoic.

Cornelius took a moment and exhaled deeply, "Sure. I will fetch him," he smiled.

With tension in the room easing, the young soldier relaxed his hand from the blade's handle. Turning to leave the room, Cornelius immediately spun back and punched the younger soldier square in the nose, only to have it crunch beneath the blow. Staggering back, Cornelius used the young soldier's momentum against him, driving him backwards toward his older comrade, knocking them both to the floor.

Flower vases shattered beneath their weight. Before either could recover and fight to their feet, Cornelius pulled the sword from the young soldier's sheath, cutting at his throat with all his strength, blood sprayed onto the nearby wall at the near decapitation.

The older soldier hardly had time to raise a hand, as he futility attempted to block the incoming attack, before the blade was thrusted through his palm, pinning his hand against his face, only to have the blade emerge out the back of his skull. In a matter of seconds both the Praetorians bodies lay limp on the floor. With his adrenaline heightened Cornelius lingered over the two bodies. Tugging at the handle, the blade released from its victim, red droplets trickled from the sword and down onto the tile flooring.

Stepping into the foyer, "What in the world is happening out...?" Floriana froze in her steps, a gasp escaping her lips as she laid eyes on her husband's face smeared with crimson blood, standing amidst the fallen soldiers at his feet.

"What did you do? Those were Augustus' men. You've doomed us for sure!" she hollered, gazing at the pool of blood gathering on the floor.

"I know, I know. Which is why we have to go now," Cornelius panted. "Have you gathered your things?"

"As soon as you told me to head to my mothers. I grabbed the pouch of coins as well. Never figured we would have to use it," Floriana said.

"That's why we have it. What about Arenius? Where is he?" he asked, kneeling down to wipe the blade clean on the soldier's garment and unfasten his hilt.

"I told him to pack for a short journey."

"Good," Cornelius said, coming to her side, kissing her on the cheek.

"Where are we going?"

"Anywhere but here. We need to get as far away as possible! But first we need to make a stop."

"But we have so mu-"

"Are they dead?" Arenius asked, entering the vestibule and cutting her words short.

"If they are no longer breathing, then they are dead," Cornelius turned to face his son. "Are you finished packing?" he asked before tossing him the dead soldier's sword.

"Yes," he replied, catching the weapon and examining it. "What's this?"

"Exactly what it looks like. Time to put what you learned to the test." Facing his son, he began to level with him, "They were not only here for me, Arenius," grabbing his gear near the door he began to put it on. "Whatever you saw or might know, Augustus wanted you too. And I could not allow it."

Arenius froze in shock, the sound of Cornelius' voice fading into the background, his gaze fixated on the lifeless figures sprawled across the entrance hall, crimson trails tracing a macabre path towards his shoes.

This can't be happening, Arenius thought, stepping back from the traveling puddle.

Following the futile endeavor to clarify matters with his father, doubt crept in, convincing him that his encounter had been nothing but a figment of his imagination. However, any inkling of disbelief dissipated as he caught wind of more unintelligible murmurs, this time emanating from the deceased warriors. As his parents engaged in hushed deliberation about their next steps, he fixated on the lifeless forms before him. It was then that he observed the same infernal smoke that had birthed the demon from Augustus' back now seeping out of the soldiers' wounds, eerily mending their torn flesh back together.

"Pa," he alerted, pointing at the bodies.

Not being able to see the smoke or hear the whispers, they turned to find the soldier's mortal wounds slowly stitch shut.

"By the gods," Floriana muttered in disbelief. A chill ran down her back.

"Whatever it is, we need to leave now," Arenius ordered,

slowly backing away.

Amazement and fear gripped they looked on as the bodies started convulsing violently. Limbs thrashed until wounds miraculously healed. Against all reason, chests rose and fell as if souls were returning from the underworld. After a tense moment, the soldiers sat upright, their eyelids flew open to reveal eyes as dark as coal.

"To the horses, now!" Cornelius ordered, grabbing a nearby lantern as they ran out of the house.

In the spacious stable, they efficiently secured the saddles onto the horses as Cornelius stood sentinel for any sign of approaching soldiers. Soon, mounted on their steeds, they departed swiftly. As they rode past the front of the home, they encountered the two Praetorian guards emerging, their armor bearing grim traces of recent combat.

Cornelius approached the soldier's horse tied to the tree outside his house. He stood at the doorway, staring at the soldiers stationed before him. A wave of disbelief swept through him. *"How can the dead walk again?"*

Lifting his sword high, he swiftly cut through the horse's reins. Using the broadside of the blade, he gave the horse a firm smack on its hindquarters, urging it to gallop away into the darkness. With their attacker's means of escape vanishing into the night, the Vesta family departed from their sanctuary without hesitation.

As they descended along the path, Arenius cast a final glance at the soldiers before they vanished from view over the hill's crest.

V

After journeying under the moon's glow for what seemed like an eternity, Arenius and Floriana trailed behind Cornelius as he led them along. In the dead of night, Arenius noticed the absence of any other soul venturing this far from Rome. The road lay deserted, devoid of travelers or vendors, with only the rhythmic clatter of their horses' hooves resonating against the cobblestones.

Cornelius veered onto a path branching to the right of the bustling main road. The narrow trail, impeccably kept, gradually grew tighter as they journeyed onward. Finally, the winding path led them to a majestic temple.

Dismounting their steeds and securing them to the designated posts near the base of the temple's steps, they discovered the surroundings enveloped in a serene hush, illuminated solely by the flickering silhouettes cast by the blazing cauldrons.

"Why we come here," Arenius asked aloud.

"Because it's our custom to do so. You're Roman, you should know that," Cornelius said, without looking at him.

Arenius moved to address the situation, but Floriana silently signaled for him to stay quiet. He deferred to her wisdom, holding his tongue, and obediently followed in step behind his parents.

Climbing the worn stone steps, the Temple of Mercury stood proudly with its iconic dome, a true embodiment of classical Roman architecture. Following the ancient Roman tradition, Cornelius felt compelled to pay homage to the god of travel before embarking on their journey, convinced that neglecting this ritual would only invite ill fate upon the traveler.

The temple stood proudly on a three-tiered pedestal, its rectangular structure adorned with four strikingly green floral Corinthian columns on the front porch. Arenius noticed the glow emanating from two bronze cauldrons placed at the feet of the outer columns, illuminating the triangular pediment perched high above the entrance. The pediment showcased a detailed frieze portraying the god Mercury engaged in diverse activities related to commerce and journeying.

Advancing through the antechamber, they crossed the threshold into the main temple, feeling as though they were stepping into a vast abyss. Each footfall reverberated through the spacious chamber, creating a haunting echo. Positioned at the center of the temple's gleaming marble floor was a bronze cauldron, its flickering flames casting dancing shadows around the magnificent statue of the temple's revered deity at the far end.

The Vesta family approached in hushed reverence, drawing closer to the towering thirty-foot figure of Mercury. The god's left hand gripped the caduceus staff, its serpents intricately entwined, while a regal bronze rooster stood proudly at his feet. Bathed in the warm glow of the cauldron's flame, the god's likeness shimmered with a golden sheen, almost as if poised to step down from its stone pedestal and come to life before their very eyes.

Cornelius and Floriana moved with a sense of urgency that

struck Arenius as unfamiliar. They swiftly navigated the temple's interior, meticulously checking for any other presence before settling in front of the statue of Mercury. Arenius followed suit, approaching Cornelius and knelt beside him.

With his loved ones gathered around him, Cornelius humbly knelt in front of the ancient statue. "Oh, revered wanderer, we beseech you for protection on our forthcoming voyage through the sacred territories destined for our tribe. May your profound insights illuminate our way and lead us towards our destined route," he concluded, the temple hushed in anticipation as he sought solace in the unyielding gaze of the stone figure.

"You are bound to run into disaster if you believe a statue is going to answer," a voice echoed in the temple's shadows.

The Vesta family sprang up as one, forming a protective circle with their weapons unsheathing simultaneously, the glint of steel reflecting in their vigilant eyes as they scanned the shadowy recesses of the temple.

"Who is there?" Cornelius shouted.

"Only a friend who wants to help," the stranger persisted, their voice a curious blend of many tones, neither distinctly male nor female.

"We will be the judge of that," Arenius blurted.

"Hold your tongue boy," Cornelius snarled, shooting a sharp glance at Arenius before returning his focus to the shifting shadows. "If your words hold weight, reveal yourself now."

As if on cue, a figure materialized from the shadows near the statue, a spot Arenius had sworn was vacant just moments before. Draped in a cloak as white as freshly fallen snow, adorned with a shimmering golden sash at the waist, their gaze obscured by a large hood.

"No need to be afraid, I mean you no harm," the stranger

gestured with their palms up.

Arenius observed intricate spiraling glyphs etched into the stranger's skin, each one shimmering in a golden ink that retained its luminosity even in the dim light.

"What are you?" Arenius chimed in.

"The question is, who are you and what do you want?" Cornelius questioned, grasping the gladius tighter.

"I am a Divine Speaker. What I am outside of that is of no concern. I have been appointed to aid you on your journey."

"What do you know about our journey? Did Augustus send you to find me?" Cornelius asked.

The Divine Speaker laughed, "We are not bothered with the quarrels of men. I was charged with coming to your son tonight."

"Did the gods guide you here?" inquired Arenius as he took a step towards the newcomer, swiftly securing his weapon at his side upon a gesture from Cornelius.

"What did I tell you, Arenius?" Cornelius barked.

"Huh, the gods? What you are kneeling before is nothing more than a pretty carved stone," continuing, the Divine Speaker moved forward, revealing more of their face as they stepped into the light, casting a glow on their unblemished features from the chin down. "I come to you by way of The One, who desires your son and others like him to fight against the growing darkness to come," circling around them, they showed no worry about the weapons in their hands.

Floriana's eyes narrowed, her grip on the sword tightening as she demanded, "And our son? How is Arenius involved in all of this?" Her weapon mirrored the Speaker's every move as they circled them.

"Yes, the protective mother with a warrior's spirit. How

fascinating," the Divine Speaker halted, his piercing gaze lingering on her as if unraveling the secrets of her soul. "The stone has awakened your son, now the essence of The One flow through him and will continue until his last breath," they assured her before facing Arenius, "Therefore Arenius, keep it close, for it is the source of your strength," the Divine Speaker's footsteps halted beneath the towering marble statue, while Arenius fixated on the ancient pendant resting against his chest.

"What? That stone?" Cornelius scoffs, glancing at the stone. "Just a trinket I haggled from a vendor in Alexandria," he remarks, sheathing his sword with a nonchalant air. Floriana mimics his actions, sliding her slender rapier back into its ornate scabbard.

"Cheap," Arenius whispered, facing Cornelius whose attention remained on the Divine Speaker.

"That is what we wanted you to believe. Not all things should be taken at face value, Tribune Cornelius, as you have witnessed in your son."

"How do you know me?" Cornelius turned his head slowly, his eyes meeting Arenius's with a curious glint.

"We know many things, such as all the blood shed across many lands by your hands. We also know of your loyalty, and the love and dedication you have for your family," the Divine Speaker responded.

"Now what about my son?" Floriana questioned again, her voice echoing in the chamber.

"Yes, Arenius has become a Light Bringer. In your tongue you may refer to them as *VIR LUCIS*, a living hero, a man of light. The ancient stone's journey spans countless lifetimes, traversing distant realms as it changes owners through the ages, until it ultimately finds its destined Light Bringer."

"You speak as though it lives," Floriana said.

"Indeed, living stones," the Divine Speaker affirmed with a subtle inclination of the head.

All attention turned towards Arenius, who remained completely absorbed in studying the intricate details of the enigmatic stone.

"No. My son has nothing to do with this new order Augustus is planning," Cornelius argued.

"I assure you; this goes beyond Augustus. Or should I say *Susru*, the demon behind Augustus that grants him his power," the Divine Speaker explained.

"Not thus again," Cornelius signed.

"Is it so hard to believe Pa, especially after what we saw back at the villa," Arenius asked.

Cornelius stood in silence, his footsteps echoing softly as he paced the room.

"Prophesy goes, when *Izraga*, the demon lord, grants Susru control of the age, the next Vir would emerge from Rome and travel to the Temple of Mercury. Where I would be ordered to give him this gladius sword, which in turn he will use to help bring balance to the known world." Unveiling the folds of their cloak, the Divine Speaker removed a gleaming sword encased in a scabbard and presented it to Arenius. Cornelius went to reach for the weapon before Arenius could react.

"No," boomed the Divine Speaker, their words echoing like thunder through the chamber. "Only the Light Bringer has the power to harness this weapon of absolute purity. In anyone else's grasp, it holds no more significance than the ordinary blade you carry now Arenius, rid yourself of that sword and embrace what fate has in store for you," they concluded, offering the weapon to him once again.

Arenius swiftly unclasped the leather strap securing the stolen gladius that once belonged to the fallen praetorian, letting it drop noiselessly to the ground. His eyes briefly met Floriana's, finding solace in her reassuring smile, before he extended his hand and firmly grasped the weapon.

"Forged from the rare and mystical Divinitium, a legendary alloy sourced from eternity, the realm of The One. Crafted into weapons or objects, its integrity is unbreakable and its sharpness everlasting. No matter the challenge, be it stone or any of earth metals, its strength is unparalleled. As its edge will retain its pristine sharpness," declared the Divine Speaker, their posture unwavering as they stood with hands concealed within their billowing sleeves.

Arenius held the weapon, observing the intricate flames etched into the silver sheath. The craftsmanship of each flame was evident in its detailed design. The handle of the blade, crafted from solid ivory, was wrapped with two delicate leather bands for a secure grip. A stunning image of a sun adorned the guard, its fiery rays enveloping the entire guard and linking to its counterpart on the opposite side.

The sword slid out of the sheath with a whisper, its obsidian blade contrasting sharply against the silver glint that danced along its edge under the soft illumination of the fire. With a series of deft twirls, he assessed its heft and equilibrium, each movement a testament to its flawless craftsmanship. This blade surpassed even the most meticulously forged weapons his father had ever acquired. More than just a tool for ending lives, it was a work of art that captivated the gaze before unleashing its deadly purpose.

Inspecting the gladius under a beam of light, he discovered a cryptic inscription etched delicately along the spine: *"Foeda Nox*

Reditum ad Nethera (Foul of the night, return to the Nether)," Arenius whispered to himself.

The craftsmanship of the weapon was exquisite, evoking tales of ancient valor and mystery. Intrigued, Arenius meticulously scrutinized every detail before noticing the small cavity within one of the intricately carved sun motifs.

"Insert the stone," insisted the Divine Speaker.

Releasing the leather strap securing the stone, he watched as it slithered down to rest by his feet. The small stone now rested in his palm, its surface catching the light and starting to emit a soft pulsating glow as he brought it nearer to the cavity. A magnetic force seemed to guide them together, and with a sudden pull, the stone slipped from his grip and seamlessly fit into the sun-shaped ivory guard.

The moment the two meet, a powerful wind and blinding light was emitted from the union of the sword and stone. Cornelius and Floriana were knocked off balance, using every ounce of their strength to stay upon their feet. Arenius stood sure amongst the intense light and strong gales coming from the stone as the Divine Speaker remained unmovable in front of him, their cloak frantically blowing about in the wind.

Returning the sword to its scabbard, the gusts of wind ceased abruptly, extinguishing the flames of the cauldron that flickered at the heart of the temple and casting the chamber into obscurity. Positioned beneath the imposing figure of Mercury, Arenius relaxed his breath, enveloped by a profound stillness that permeated the sacred space. Cornelius and Floriana stood transfixed, unable to articulate their astonishment at the spectacle they had just beheld, a manifestation that solidified the proclamations of the Divine Speaker.

Floriana was first to run to Arenius' side, "Are you all right?"

she asked, frantically checking him over.

"I feel great," Arenius responded euphorically.

"What did you do to him?" Cornelius questioned, facing the Divine Speaker.

"What you ask is irrelevant to the cause, for they are here," The Divine Speaker gestured gracefully, a flick of their fingers reigniting the cauldron in front of them.

"Who's here?" Cornelius asked.

"They go by many names; *Set, Dimme, Tiamat, yokai, Rakasa*. But in your tongue, they are the *Daemones*. Demons spawn, hell bent on controlling the world of mankind. They prefer to remain unnoticed, working in the shadows by possessing the bodies of those who are weak-minded. In this form they can only be seen and detected by Light Bringers. Though, strong demons may expose their true form."

"This cannot be true, they are myths to keep society at bay," Cornelius argued.

"Go on, inform them," The Divine Speaker said calmly, gesturing towards the grand doors of the ancient temple looming in the background.

Turning to face the temple the door, the Vesta's were met by three Praetorian guards, their presence ominous as they stood stoically in the moonlit doorway. Among the three were two familiar figures, the two guards dispatched by Augustus to their home.

"So, all my son has been telling me is true," Cornelius acknowledged, pulling out his sword.

"You wanted him to be different, now he is," Floriana said, her attention fixed on the soldier while also freeing her blade from its sheath.

Assuming his battle stance, "Let's see if your fighting matches your promises," Cornelius said.

Receiving no reply, he glanced around only to discover the Divine Speaker had vanished without a trace.

"The proximity of danger is signaled by the blade's radiant glow," concluded the Divine Speaker, their words resonating as if carried on ethereal whispers that dissolved into the darkness.

With no options or a place to run, Arenius fastened the sheath around his waist and removed his weapon to find the silver coated blade glowing purple. Feeling a sense of purpose rise up within him, he grabbed the sword with both hands and stepped out from between his parents, taking position at the front.

Empowered by a surge of energy, Arenius fixed his gaze on the soldiers advancing cautiously into the ancient temple, their weapons glinting menacingly in the dim light, their eyes smoldering with determination. Cornelius and Floriana exchanged a quick glance, marveling at the newfound assurance radiating from Arenius as he wielded the supernatural sword.

"There is nowhere for you to go, Tribune. Surrender the boy, and your wife will meet a swift and dignified end. As for you, expect to be delivered back to Caesar," the old guard commanded, halting their advance right at the entrance of the temple.

"As my sword answered you before. No," Cornelius barked.

Laughing, "I assume the Divine Speaker said something to boost your morale. However, you of all people know, no is not an option when it comes to Augustus," glancing at the other two soldiers, "End them!"

The two soldiers surged forward with lightning speed, swiftly converging on Cornelius and Floriana in a blur of motion. As the intense battle unfolded around the crackling cauldron, Arenius maintained his defensive position, his gaze unwaveringly fixed on their commanding officer.

Arenius tightened his grip on the weapon, urgency pulsing through him, *"I need to end this quickly. And send a message to Augustus, to leave my family alone,"* Arenius thought.

VI

Muscles coiled with an unfamiliar fervor, Arenius sensed a primal drive surging through him. Instinct took over as he vaulted skyward, easily spanning the fiery pit below to close in on the seasoned praetorian. Brandishing his gladius aloft, a battle cry erupted from deep within him as he unleashed a mighty strike fueled by sheer determination.

The world around them seemed to slow as Arenius made the daring leap across the temple, the old Praetorian stood motionless, his eyes fixed on his opponent. With a swift and graceful movement, Arenius propelled himself forward, his blade inches away from the soldier's face. But the soldier was ready for him, drawing his gladius from its sheath with lightning speed and blocking Arenius' attack. The clash of metal echoed through the temple as they engaged in a fierce duel, sparks flying every time their swords met.

Arenius hovered mid-air, their swords clashing fiercely. With a swift strike, Arenius pushed the guard skidding back out of the Temple's door. As they both paused, locking eyes, a wry smile crept onto the old Praetorian's face before effortlessly deflecting Arenius' attack. In a sudden motion of the Praetorian's sword, Arenius was hurled backward, soaring fifteen feet until crashing into one of the massive interior columns. The impact twisted and bent Arenius around the solid stone pillar, each spine-jarring crack reverberating through his body. Finally, with a thunderous crash, Arenius plummeted eight feet to the ground as chunks of marble rained down upon them.

Sheathing his weapon with a swift motion, the old Praetorian sprinted across the temple with uncanny agility. In a blur of movement, he seized Arenius by the neck, hoisting him off the ground and forcefully pinning him against the pillar. His grip was vice-like, constricting Arenius' air supply as he drew him in close, their faces nearly touching.

"Is this all you have for us?" laughed the Praetorian, his breath warm to Arenius' face.

"Do all demons talk this much," Arenius growled through clenched teeth.

Arenius seized the opportunity to strike, swiftly raising his gleaming sword towards his opponent. The Praetorian, unfazed, intercepted the attack by grabbing Arenius' wrist with a firm grip. "Nice try," he smiled, slamming Arenius' hand against the column to free the blade.

Arenius's knuckles redden as he clenched the gladius, its weight a familiar comfort in his grip. With each brutal strike from the guard, the impact reverberated through his bones, jarring his teeth together. Blood trickled down his knuckles, as he worked to maintain his grip.

"Your weapon is an extension of you," Arenius could hear the words of his father replaying in his head.

With every forceful blow, crimson ribbons unfurled from his battered knuckles, painting a macabre masterpiece on the unyielding stone surface, carving intricate patterns of agony into the pillar.

"I will not lose my weapon," Despite the relentless barrage of

strikes, Arenius mustered all his willpower to uplift his spirits. However, as his strength waned, the gladius slipped from his grip and resonated loudly upon hitting the stone floor.

"Good," teased the old Praetorian as he squeezed Arenius' windpipe closed. "Do not worry, it will all be over shortly."

Arenius relentlessly pounded his fist against the guard's unyielding forearm, each strike reverberating through his arm. The Praetorian's grip was like a vice, crushing the air from Arenius' lungs. Despite the suffocating pressure, he summoned every ounce of strength within him. This was his moment to break free from the shackles of defeat.

"Always look death in the eye. It may take you, but it can never take your honor," he recalled the words Cornelius repeated to him often.

With his gaze locked with the Praetorian's, he discerned within their eyes only a seething mix of malice, jealousy, and twisted satisfaction.

"His eyes!" Arenius thought as the realization came to him.

In an instant, he thrust his thumbs viciously into the Praetorian's eyes, eliciting a sharp cry of agony before the guard retaliated with a powerful punch to Arenius' stomach. The impact felt like it could have pierced through his sternum, brushing against the solid column behind him. Before Arenius could even gasp for breath, the guard lifted and ruthlessly slammed him into the ground, shattering tiles and forming a small crater beneath his body.

"You'll rue the day you decided to do that, lad," the Praetorian roared, vigorously massaging his eyes to dispel the blurriness.

In a swift move, Arenius rolled a few paces away taking in deep breaths of air. The old Praetorian drew his gladius from its scabbard, his eyes ablaze with a fiery intensity that spoke of deep-seated animosity.

"Arenius," shouted Cornelius, upon seeing his son being flung to the temple's floor.

Cornelius rushed towards Arenius for help, but the swift young soldier he was engaged with swiftly blocked his path, and disrupting his line of sight.

"We're far from finished, Tribune," the young soldier sneered, launching a relentless flurry of strikes that left Cornelius with no choice but to engage, as he evades or deflects each blow.

Slowly pacing toward Arenius, "Some strength you have there, boy. But do you think I survived countless battles and defeated numerable foes, to be defeated by a failure of a son such as yourself? Becoming a Vir is not enough to save you or your family," the old Praetorian hissed through clenched teeth.

Struggling to rise, Arenius's body trembled as he pushed himself up from the cold stone floor, a metallic taste of blood filling his mouth. His gaze fixed on his parents locked in a fierce dance of blades with the other Praetorian Guards. The clash of steel echoed through the chamber like thunder, sparks flying as each strike was met with expert parries and counterattacks. He was amazed at how his parents were able to defend off the guards who were moving with lethal precision, which spoke of years of training.

"Yes, their struggle will end soon as well," the Praetorian taunting.

Floriana's movements were a dance of lethal precision. With each swing of her sword, the blade sliced through the air with a whispering hiss, leaving behind a trail of shimmering silver in its wake. Her footwork was agile and swift, as she pivoted on her heel, seamlessly transitioning from defense to offense. And with a determined face, she slashed at her opponent like a panther stalking its prey in the dense jungle undergrowth.

Cornelius transformed into a lion, his predatory instincts guiding his every move as he assessed his opponent for the decisive strike. Arenius, was witnessing his father's combat prowess for the first time, seeing only unwavering focus on Cornelius' face. The fluidity of Cornelius' defenses and attacks displayed a mastery of swordsmanship. That is when, Cornelius delivered a powerful blow to the young Praetorian's right side, momentarily exposing his vulnerable chest. As the soldier staggered back, falling to his knees in pain, clutching his wound, Cornelius felt a surge of triumph. However, to his astonishment, the fallen soldier rose again with a smirk, eager to continue the fight.

At that moment, Arenius came to the stark realization that despite his parents' formidable skills as warriors, they lacked the power to banish the malevolent demons within the soldiers.

"Foul of the night, return to the Nether," Arenius whispered to himself.

"That's right boy, cry out to The One for help. But let me tell you a secret, help's not coming," the Praetorian teased.

"Foul of the night, return to the Nether," Arenius's voice boomed, cutting through the chaos around them, ensuring the soldier couldn't miss his words."

The wrinkles etched around the Old Praetorian's eyes deepened, erasing the remnants of a smile that once graced his weathered face, "You'll be long gone before you can utter those words again. Being chosen does not mean you are special. It simply means The One wasted more power on your useless flesh," he growled, as he towered over Arenius, raising his sword to deliver the final blow.

The soldier's sword descended with a menacing glint, slicing through the air like a vengeful comet as Arenius stood poised, his breath steady despite the imminent danger. Anticipating the strike, he moved with a fluid grace evading the lethal arc by a hair's breadth. The ground accepted his weight in a whisper of dust.

Rising swiftly to his knees, Arenius seized his sword with a firm grip, feeling its familiar weight anchor him in the chaos of battle. With a fierceness blazing in his eyes, he brought the blade upward, cutting through the air with an almost musical swiftness. A trail of iridescent purple light followed the arc of his weapon like a mystical ribbon unfurling behind a shooting star.

The aftermath of his swift strike lingered briefly in the air, a trail of light marking the path of his sword as it sliced through the darkness. A thud echoed through the chamber as the old Praetorian's forearm hit the stone floor. Clutching the amputated limb, he growled in agony.

Arenius, fueled by the will to save his parents, he seized the opportunity presented. A with a fluid motion, he unleashed a powerful spin attack to cleanly severing the old Praetorian's head from his body. The headless corpse crumpled to the unforgiving ground of the temple, lifeless eyes staring into eternity.

As if scripted by fate itself, both head and body began to disintegrate in a mesmerizing display of shimmering light. The remnants of their existence dissolved into nothingness, leaving behind only a lingering aura of light before fading completely.

Upon hearing the anguished cries of their leader, the two guards whipped around in disbelief. How could someone so youthful overpower one of their seasoned comrades? Their momentary pause proved fatal. Arenius swiftly flung his gladius towards the assailant of his mother. The blade sank deep into the guard's chest, causing him to disintegrate into shimmering particles, while the weapon clattered to the ground. Witnessing this turn of events, the last guard made a desperate dash for the exit, only to be pursued by Cornelius who ruthlessly struck at his leg, sending him crashing down. Retrieving his gladius, Arenius ran after Cornelius as they exited the temple.

"Please don't do this," begged the young soldier. "I can tell you things. I can tell you what Augustus is planning," the remaining soldier pleaded, as he shuffled awkwardly on his back as the Vesta family encircled him.

"You coming to hurt my family and I says enough," Arenius said through clenched, his eyes blazed with anger as he lunged forward.

The blade found its mark in the praetorian guard's armor, cutting through metal and flesh with a sickening sound. With a swift motion, he withdrew the sword, watching as the last enemy vanished into a cascade of light.

"Why'd you do that? He was about to tell us of Augustus' plan," Cornelius yelled in frustration.

"Because I had to. You did not have to watch while you and Ma had no way of defeating them. It is what I was called to do, whether you believe it or not. You no longer have to see me as your worthless son," Arenius argued, then headed down the temple steps for their horses.

"Arenius! Stand at attention!" Cornelius yelled, chasing after his son.

Arenius paused, "Oh, now you're angry at me for doing what you beat in me to do all these years. Which one is it, Pa? Or, are you really mad because I was able to defeat them and you were not able to come out the hero as always?"

Arenius pushed on and reaching their horses at the bottom of the temple's steps, he began to unhitch the horses.

"When I give you an order, you listen," Cornelius continued.

"Well, it is a good thing I am not one of your soldiers to be ordered around," Arenius continued his task, his gaze fixed ahead.

Cornelius extended his hand towards Arenius' shoulder, the fabric of his robe rustling softly as he moved. Before his touch could land, Arenius spun around with a fluid grace, seizing Cornelius' wrist in a swift and assertive motion.

"Don't you dare think about touching me," Arenius's grip on Cornelius' wrist tightened like a vise. Despite Cornelius's attempts to break free, Arenius' hold remained unyielding, locking them in a tense stare-down as their eyes locked in a silent battle of wills. "The boy you thought you controlled is no more," he ended, shoving his hand away.

Floriana swiftly caught Cornelius as he staggered backwards, and for a moment they exchanged astonished glances at their son's display of strength. Without a word, Arenius hesitated briefly before silently turning on his heels and departing.

"Arenius, mind yourself. He is your father," Floriana yelled.

Arenius faced them, "Is he? When has he ever been a father to me? Is he a father, when he looks upon me in shame? Or is he a father when he thinks I cannot even go to the markets without messing things up. Or was he a father, before or after him leaving us for so many years?"

Silence greeted Arenius as he reclaimed his horse. Meeting his father's gaze, he asserted, "Well, just like then, I can handle myself, and we do not need you as much as you think!" With determination in his eyes, he spurred his steed into a swift gallop along the shadowy path, swiftly distancing himself from them.

VII

Only a few hours lingered before dawn, and the Vestas had forgone food, rest, and respite since facing the demons at the Temple of Mercury. Arenius withdrew into solitude, his mind consumed with unraveling the upheaval that had overtaken his world. In particular his lack of remorse after ending the lives of those soldiers.

He always expected his first at ending a life would be more difficult than it was, yet he felt nothing. Was it because they were no longer human, and merely a shell of their former selves? He asked himself, over and over, should it have been more difficult or easier to end another's life?

Questions swirled in his mind like a tempest, each one a sharp gust threatening to derail his journey as a Vir. The elusive answers he sought were the key to unlocking his potential, yet the path to obtaining them remained shrouded in mystery, leaving him adrift in uncertainty.

"Cornelius, we cannot go on like this," Floriana's voice barely rose above a murmur, shattering the oppressive quiet that enveloped them. Pausing briefly, she stole a quick glance towards Arenius, who rode a few paces ahead, confirming their privacy before continuing their hushed exchange. "Where are we going?"

Lost in a haze of contemplation, Cornelius mirrored his son's distraction, rendering his wife's words unheard. He pressed on, fixated straight ahead at his boy.

"Cornelius!" Floriana exclaimed, bringing her horse to an abrupt halt.

His eyes widened, a sudden jolt of realization he had been ignoring her. "Yes, my love," turning the horse around, leaving Arenius to himself. "I am sorry."

"Look at yourself. You are exhausted. You are unfocused. I'm not even sure if you know where we are heading," she questioned.

Recognizing the truth in her words, he urged, "We have to keep moving. The longer we linger on this shore, our safety is at risk."

"Well, can you tell me where are we going?" Floriana asked anxiously.

"To Ostia," he replied.

"Ostia? That's more than a day's journey!" She asked.

"Which gives us more of a reason to keep moving, and stay ahead," he promptly responded.

"How are we to do that without rest or food? And what about Arenius? You haven't said a word to him since the temple. Yet you're not able to take your eyes off of him."

"He doesn't want to talk. So, I let him be," Cornelius said with little emotion.

"Damn it, Cornelius. He's your son, of course he wants to talk," Floriana argued. "You need to stop treating him like he's one of your grunts and maybe you could get somewhere."

"I have," Cornelius suggested, sitting tall on his horse.

"No, you have not!" she contested, releasing his hand, "And if you have, its only when making a soldier. You've been training, but he doesn't need training, right now he needs you," she ended peering into his eyes.

Cornelius sighed and smiled, bringing his horse closer to her side. Gazing upon her olive face. "You're going to be the death of me yet," he jested, leaning in and giving her a kiss on the forehead.

"Fix this, she continued," Floriana said, leaning away from him.

"I'll do my best, I promi—"

"Ma, Pa!" Arenius belted from around the bend in the road, cutting his words short.

"Arenius!" They exclaimed in unison before dashing off to find their son.

Urging their weary steeds to their limits, the horses' hooves pounded against the ancient cobblestones. Rounding the corner, they came upon Arenius, who had dismounted and was crouched next to the splintered wheel of a dilapidated flatbed carriage, with a frail elderly woman by his side.

"What is it?" Cornelius asked, bringing his horse to a stop behind them.

"Arenius, are you ok?" Floriana said.

"What's wrong," Cornelius asked in unison

Perplexed by their excessive caution, Arenius studied their every move with growing curiosity. "I'm unharmed. No danger," he reassured, casting a quick glance at his father. "This lady requires our assistance."

"Gratitude fills me; encountering compassionate souls like yours is a rarity in these times. I never anticipated aid at this late hour. I go by Cecilia," she introduced herself, approaching Cornelius with a linen cloak draped around her, warding off the cold night breeze. "Few venture these paths in the dead of night.

It's a risk, for one never knows who lurks nearby. Yet here I am, with goods to carry," she mentioned, attempting to stroke his horse, but it shied away.

Steadying his horse, Cornelius pointed out, "I see that's not deterring you from venturing on," as he observed the woman closely, noting the weathered complexion that hinted at days spent under the intense Mediterranean sun.

With a courteous smile, "With the abundance of goods in my possession and the urgency to reach Ostia before daybreak, fear of highway robbers is a luxury I cannot entertain. Besides, the Consul's efforts have undeniably improved the safety of all public roads."

Surveying the split wheel, "I'm sorry, ma'am, but we're not able to assist. We have matters of our own to attend to," Cornelius withdrew, knowing it would take some time to repair the damage. "There is a military encampment about four miles ahead, I'm sure they could be of some assistance."

"Wait a moment. Your son assured help. And I cannot abandon my entire livelihood, laid out vulnerably on this path, for any rogue to snatch away. If only I had a robust young fellow like you, this predicament would not even arise," Cecilia implored as she emerged into the glow cast by a flickering torch fastened to her carriage.

"Please forgive my son. Sometimes he takes on issues that are too big for him," Cornelius assured her.

"Pa, we can't just stand by," Arenius whispered urgently as he moved closer.

"Arenius, I understand your intentions to act with integrity, but our attention is needed elsewhere," Cornelius whispered sternly and cautiously, mindful of potential eavesdroppers.

"I understand, but it's been hours since we last saw or heard anything from them. There's no indication of any demon activity," he reassured, drawing his gladius halfway to display its usual shine. "Look, no glow," he pointed out before carefully sliding the blade back into its scabbard. "She seems weary from her journey, and is seeking assistance. With my newfound skills, aiding her will be swift. If I can't assist an elderly traveler in need, how can I fulfill my destined purpose?"

Looking into his son's clear blue eyes, Cornelius pondered the purity he saw there and the weight of Floriana's promise to rectify the situation. "Very well. However, should circumstances shift, we depart without delay. Your mother and you are my top priority, above all others. Is that understood?"

"Agreed," Arenius answered with a smile.

"While you both attend to the carriage, I'll take this opportunity to unwind and perhaps explore if there's any food available," Floriana chimed in, as she gracefully dismounted from her horse.

"Let's not get too comfortable, we need to remain—," Cornelius whispered, his voice barely audible.

"I'm familiar with the routine, my dear," she interjected, her tone brisk. "Instead of berating me, you could help your son, you know," she continued, securing the horse to a sturdy sapling by the roadside before searching around the carriage for Cecilia. "Cornelius, my husband, and Arenius, my son, are seeing to your carriage," she said, finding Cecelia further inspecting her carriage.

"Oh, great be the gods. I wasn't sure what I was going to do. What can I do to repay you? I have a couple sestertius," she offered, slowly turning to the front of the carriage, "I know it's not much but...,"

"Do no such thing. You keep your coin," Floriana said, "But we would appreciate some food and water if you have it to spare?"

"My dear, where are my manners? I have plenty, come with me," she said, linking her arm with Floriana's and leading her towards the front of the carriage. "Packed more than enough for the journey to Ostia, to peddle my goods on the back," she continued, she shared, gesturing towards the array of merchandise on the carriage's flatbed. "The food in Ostia would cost you two days' wages, don't get me started on an Inn," Cecilia laughed, reaching for something on her front seat.

"Ostia? That's our destination too," Floriana added.

"Look at that. The gods do work mysteriously, don't they?" Cecilia said while handing Floriana a large water gourd.

"Sure do," taking and drinking from the gourd. "Much needed, thanks."

"It's fresh from the aqueduct. Be sure to save your son and husband some," she smiled, as they both glance at Arenius and Cornelius working on the repair. "You sure do have a beautiful family. And a strong son might I add," seeing Arenius lift the carriage alone, while Cornelius removed the wheel. "Your husband and son work well with each other; they must be close?"

"Yes, he's a growing boy," taking uncomfortable sip from the container. "We are a happy family but them working together, that's a different story entirely."

"Why is that?"

"My husband spent much time in the military. And being a soldier, he has a certain way, let's say, of seeing what makes a man. With that, he pushes my son to be the best he can be. Sometimes, just a little too hard," Floriana ended, her eyes locked on the two important men in her life, working together.

It did her heart good to see them, this way, no grueling sweat, or blood. In that moment, they were father and son, the way she always dreamed it would be.

"Family is a very delicate thing, and the smallest of things have the potential to bring ruin. How do I know? Well, like I said, there is a reason I'm old and traveling alone," she paused briefly to eat a few dried dates from a bag. "Yet we have one life to live and it's up to us to live it," Cecilia said, tossing another date into her mouth.

"There," Arenius said, beaming with pride as Cornelius secured the wheel, enabling him to lower the carriage back onto the earth with gentle precision.

"This remarkable talent of yours is truly extraordinary, reducing the workload of four men by half," Cornelius exclaimed proudly, his hand resting on Arenius' shoulder. "The carriage itself is as heavy as two horses and you made it look as though you were lifting a feather. We're going to have to keep an eye on what else you can do, to discover the full extent of your abilities," he added. "There's no need to linger here any longer. Our work is complete," he informed the rest of the group.

"Already?" Cecilia said, approaching them. "It would have taken my husband hours to even get the wheel off. And you did it before I could even offer you a drink of water. Now that's something else."

"Here, take this," Floriana extended a carved wooden gourd filled with cool, clear water towards him.

"Shall I prepare a hearty meal for all of us, and we can stay here tonight before journeying to Ostia tomorrow as a group?" Cecilia suggested while Arenius and Cornelius shared sips of water from the gourd. "It will give you and your animals a chance to recuperate. I've got all the essentials to start a fire."

"Who said we are going to Ostia?" Cornelius asked, as Cecelia's eyes quickly glance guided him to Floriana.

"What, girl talk," Floriana shrugged.

"Apologies, Ma'am, but it's time for us to depart," Cornelius stated firmly, his gaze unwaveringly fixed on hers.

"Cornelius, as much as I would love to get back on that horse, I have to agree with her. We have to rest and eat. Arenius may be able to go on but I can't. It's been years since I've rode throughout the night. I need to rest, love, and so do you."

"Fantastic, just what we needed," Cornelius muttered, his eyes rolling in exasperation. "Arenius and I will seek out a clearing."

Taking one of the burning torches from the carriage and with Arenius at his side, the two headed into the woods.

VIII

Nestled deep within the intricate labyrinth of a stone pine forest, where moonlight filters through the dense network of branches like golden threads, a secluded clearing harbors a solitary campfire. The flames dance and flicker, casting ethereal shadows that playfully intertwine with the enveloping darkness. Cecelia skillfully tends to the fire, the crackling flames embracing chunks of mysterious salted meat skewered on makeshift roasting sticks. As the savory aroma mingles with the earthy scent of pine, her companions gather around the fire's welcoming glow, reclining on soft blankets woven by Cecelia's hands.

Under the twinkling canopy of stars and amidst a gentle but cool summer breeze rustling the leaves, Arenius honed in on the symphony of wildlife sounds. As dappled light played on his youthful features, he savored each bite of roasted meat only to wash it down with cool water. All while contemplating and recounting the events of his transformative day.

Within a single day, his familiar world had been completely upended. His initial desire had been simple: to bond with his father and gain his approval. Yet, as a Vir now fleeing for survival alongside his family, he questioned the value of this newfound status. The abrupt transition from their cherished home to a life on the run, relying on the charity of a stranger deep in the forest, made him ponder whether the pursuit of greatness was truly worth the sacrifice.

"What's next, to be forever on the run? Is power and respect worth this way of life?" He questioned himself.

"What's taking you and your family to Ostia," Cecelia asked Arenius a few feet away, breaking him from his trance-like stare.

Arenius glanced across the fire at Cornelius and Floriana who were wrapped in their own conversation.

Taking a moment to gather his thoughts, *"Ah,* I'm not sure. I guess my father wanted to spend some time together before his next tour," he replied, glancing up from the fire at his parents again.

"He sure does carry the aura of a distinguished soldier. Where did he serve?"

"You should be asking where he didn't," Arenius mumbled.

"What was that?"

"Never mind," shaking the thought away. "He received most of his honors at the Battle of Actium."

"I thought his name was familiar. It was said under the direct command of Augustus Caesar, he led the decisive charge against the traitor Mark Anthony and the barbarian Queen Cleopatra," Cecelia marveled.

"The gods be praised, the Hero of Actium, across from us," Arenius responded sarcastically.

"It must be hard living up to someone like him," she stood, being sure to grab the nearby water gourd.

"That's putting it lightly. It's like no matter how hard I try, nothing is ever good enough for him. And when I do have the chance in a lifetime to prove myself, nothing I say matters. In his world it's like I don't exist."

"I'm sure he means well," she approached, refilling his cup. "Sometimes seasons pass before people are able to see what really makes us," she said with a wink, then made her way towards the others.

"Perhaps," he murmured. With a final sip, he carefully concealed his sword under his blanket before settling down on his back. Gazing up at the star-studded sky, he lingered until drowsiness weighed down his eyelids.

"Ostia is our best bet of leaving the mainland quickly," Cornelius whispered, seeing Cecelia approaching.

"Apologies for the interruption, but I thought it might be nice to fill everyone's drinks before sleep overthrows me. These days, staying awake into the wee hours is a rarity for me. My departed spouse used to tease that my demeanor suffered when I was tired."

"Thank you, Cecelia," Floriana acknowledged.

"The pleasure is all mine, to serve such nice people."

"We are grateful to have your company tonight," Floriana added, raising her glass to be filled, Cornelius doing the same.

"Well, it was a long day. Time to lay this old body down. You two sleep well," Cecelia finished heading back to her blanket.

"What a nice woman, reminds me of my mother," Floriana said.

"Your mother being nice, is like saying Tartarus is paradise," Cornelius joked, receiving a quick jab from Floriana.

"Don't talk about my mother. Keep saying such things and her spirit may decide to visit you one day."

"Alright, I'll leave your dear mother to rest in peace," he diverted the conversation. He paused to take a sip from his cup, reclining on his elbows. "Returning to my point, our route starts in Ostia where we can board a ship bound for Tarsus. Once in Tarsus, an acquaintance will assist us in navigating beyond Republic borders," he continued, noticing that his speech was starting to slur slightly.

Fixing his gaze on Florianna, who seemed to split into three before slumping over onto his lap, unconscious.

"Floriana," he called out weakly, trying unsuccessfully to rouse her. "What's happen—?" he muttered, staring blankly into his cup as darkness crept over him.

Unconscious, Arenius was swiftly transported to the astral plane, a realm bridging the human world and the Netherworld. Mirroring his previous experience, he observed his physical form resting on a blanket in the forest, gazing up at the sky. On the other side of the crackling fire, his parents conversed animatedly. Struggling to discern their words, he was enveloped by the roaring of a nearby river, distorting their voices as if they were submerged underwater.

Before he could study them further, he found himself hurtling across the terrain at a speed far surpassing any horseback ride he had experienced. In an instant, a blur of trees, mountains, expansive plains, deep valleys, rivers, and unfamiliar territories whizzed past him, where the sun and moon seemed to rise and set multiple times in rapid succession. What would have been a journey spanning weeks on either horse or boat was now traversed in what seemed like mere moments.

Although traveling the astral plane alone, Arenius couldn't shake the sensation for the presence of another, howbeit, non-threatening.

Gradually, the flow of time and pace reverted to their usual rhythm; under the moonlit sky, he glided effortlessly like a majestic hawk riding a balmy current. Despite the tumultuous waves churning below, not a hint of moisture or wind touched him. Traveling vast distances through the night, a beacon of light materialized on the far-off horizon. As he drew nearer to this illumination, a colossal tower emerged from the depths of the sea, its structure ascending towards the heavens with a fierce inferno ablaze atop it, casting its brilliance across the shadowy expanse.

Flying over the tower, he navigated through a sprawling city filled with sturdy stone houses and winding roads. At the outskirts, a majestic palace perched atop a hill overlooked the bustling market-place where vendors hawked an array of goods. Dominating the cityscape was a grand temple adorned with eleven colossal statues of gods carved from stone, each standing guard at its entrances. The central statue, towering above the rest, portrayed a bearded man with intricate curly hair.

Arenius found himself standing before an impressive temple-like structure adorned with six towering fifty-foot marble columns that stood guard in front of a grand thirty-foot wooden door. As he approached, the massive doors creaked open, welcoming him into a vast chamber bustling with scholars representing diverse empires. The interior was a maze of shelves overflowing with ancient scrolls, each holding secrets and knowledge sought by these faceless seekers. Navigating through the throng of scholars, Arenius eventually reached a nondescript shelf at the back of the room where he discovered a carving in the wood that bore a striking resemblance to his own stone

Arenius reached out to touch the object when a voice suddenly called his name, "Arenius, awaken," the commanding yet soothing voice resonated as if it came from all around him.

Whirling around in anticipation of encountering a presence lurking behind him, he discovered instead a group of scholars lost in their own realms, engrossed in their academic pursuits without a care for what he might have overheard.

"Arise," the ethereal voice echoed once more, beckoning Arenius as he was pulled back across all the lands he crossed. Soaring across the city, gliding over the blazing tower, skimming above the expansive sea, fields, and valleys, until he descended back into the confines of his physical form.

IX

Arenius woke in a frenzy; not of fear, but in excitement for his second experience, only to find himself surrounded by the serene stillness of the nocturnal forest. The fleeting warmth of the crackling fire beside him couldn't stave off an eerie feeling. Surveying his surroundings, he noticed everything appeared normal until he tried to rise and realized his hands and feet were tightly bound by rough rope. A shiver raced down his spine, sending a wave of cold through him under the vast starlit sky. While the once lively forest fell into an eerie silence, as though every creature in it had sensed a hidden threat nearby.

"Ma, Pa!" he called out in a hushed tone, pivoting towards the vacant spots where they had sat moments ago. Only to finding their absence, his gaze shifted to the other side. "Cecelia!" his voice carried softly, confirming her absence too.

Fighting against his ropes, Arenius began to feel something he thought he had overcome - fear.

"How could I be afraid, I'm a Light Bringer," he questioned himself.

Panic surged within him, seizing his emotions. He resisted the restraints, each tug causing the ropes to strip away slivers of skin from his wrists and ankles. The darkness enveloping him seemed to murmur with silent voices. Arenius abruptly ceased his struggles, scanning the shadows for any elusive movements in the forest beyond the flickering firelight.

A low, guttural voice rumbled from the darkness behind Arenius, "I had been anticipating the awakening of the boy Light Bringer."

"Who are you?" Arenius inquired, his eyes darting around as he sought the unseen presence.

"No one escapes Susru," the voice continued.

"Pa, Pa!" Arenius called once more.

"I can hear the fear curdling in your voice boy, and its invigorating," the voice laughed menacingly. "Know that fear is only a taste of what's to come."

"Ma, Pa!" Arenius called out once more.

"I doubt your parents will come looking for you. You're on your own, little one," the eerie voice declared, its chilling tone originating from the far end of the woods.

"How are they moving so fast?" Arenius thought, his eyes attempting to follow the bouncing voice. "What did you do with my parents?" he barked.

"Don't worry, Susru has plans for the great Tribune Cornelius. Your mother, however, let's just say, she's on the cutting board as we speak."

"You touch them and I'll–"

"You'll what, continue to call out to your parents," their voice boomed, cutting Arenius' words short. "You'll lay there until I decide how I want to dispose of you."

"Stop the chatter and show yourself," Arenius ordered.

"It'll be my pleasure."

The forest hushed, and Arenius strained his ears to the sound of twigs snapping in the distance. Slow footsteps drew nearer, breaking the silence. His gaze fixed on a shadowy area, he watched as the steps approached, revealing a towering figure illuminated by the flickering firelight. Clad in the distinctive black armor of the Praetorian Guard, the individual stood at six feet tall, casually bearing a hefty twenty-two-pound scutum shield by their side. Their identity concealed behind an iron mask and helmet.

In the flickering glow of the campfire, the soldier's muscular arms were accentuated by the dancing light. Silent and cornered, Arenius launched into a desperate struggle against his bonds. Initially futile, his efforts gained traction as strands of the rope started to give way as he fought against them. A glimmer of hope ignited within him at the sight of the weakening fibers. Summoning all his remaining strength, he pushed through until the rope finally gave in, unraveling in a cascade of threads. With nimble hands, he seized the gladius hidden beneath his cloak and swiftly cut through the bindings securing his feet.

"Where are my parents?" Arenius demanded, springing to his feet to face his foe.

"*Aah*, you may not be the loser Susru claimed you to be. I could have ended you in your sleep but what honor is in that? I needed to know what the son of General Cornelius could do," he teased, his words muffled by the deadpan stare mask. "Let's see what an awakened Light Bringer is capable of."

Disappearing like a wraith, the Praetorian soldier melted into the darkness, leaving no trace behind.

Arenius, uncertain of the soldier's whereabouts, assumed a defensive posture. His fingers tightened around the hilt of his gladius as he pivoted in a fluid motion, ensuring no blind spot was left unguarded. Focusing intently, he extended the blade forward, its radiant purple light illuminating the surroundings. With vigilant eyes scanning every shadow, he braced himself for the anticipated attack. When it finally came, it caught him off guard in an unexpected manner.

Despite being a Light Bringer, he lacked the power to see through the shrouds of darkness enveloping him. The hairs on his neck rose in warning, signaling the presence of his relentless assailant lurking within. And yet, even in the veil, he could feel the Praetorian's eyes locked on him.

Out of the shadows, as swift as a hunting falcon, the Praetorian's shield sliced through the air towards Arenius with deadly precision. In that heart-stopping moment, time stretched on, granting Arenius a split-second to pivot to his right. The massive twenty-two-pound shield whizzed past his ear, embedding itself deeply into an umbrella pine tree behind him, nearly slicing it into. A resonant buzz reverberated through the tranquil forest, the shield's metallic song lingering in the stillness.

"Nice reflexes," the Praetorian cackled from the shadows, "Let's see what else you can do."

Swift as a fleeting shadow, the Praetorian burst out of the dense forest, catching Arenius off guard with a lightning-quick punch to his jaw. Before Arenius could fully register what had happened, the guard vanished back into the darkness. Shaking off the surprise blow, Arenius readied himself once more, only to be struck again by a sudden gust of wind, this time from an unexpected angle. Helpless against these rapid and unseen assaults, he found himself unable to anticipate or defend against the elusive attacker's relentless strikes.

A fierce strike struck Arenius's chest, propelling him in a graceful arc over the crackling campfire. He hit the ground with a resounding thud on the far side, executing a swift roll that seamlessly transitioned into a fluid rise to his feet. His weapon extended before him, poised for combat against an unseen adversary. But as he scanned the surroundings, there was only eerie silence greeting his readiness.

"How can someone that size move so fast?" Arenius questioned himself, saliva and blood oozing from his busted mouth.

"I thought a Vir from the Vesta bloodline would be more worthy of a fight. Especially after ending Susru's scout troops at the temple of Mercury," the Praetorian Guard chuckled. "But you're just a scared little boy. A boy who will die all alone in this forsaken forest. Maybe not alone, as your corpse will feed scavenging beast roaming the night."

"You know nothing of me," Arenius roared.

Stalking Arenius from the darkness, "Oh, we know much of you my young friend. You live in the shadow of your father, failing his expectations, only to crawl and be cradled in your Spartan mother's arms. How is that?" Unable to deny, Arenius allow the crackling fire to respond for him. "I thought so."

"What do you want," Arenius snapped?"

"It's simple. To have the Vir dead, marking Susru's complete rule over the civilized world immanent."

"Rome has no king," said Arenius, focusing his senses to scan the area for where the next strike may come from.

"How wrong you are again. The Great Julius Caesar laid the groundwork for his nephew. With that, Susru will sit upon the greatest seat in the world. And we, his praetorian guard, will be at his side to make sure he stays as such."

"You'll have to send my soul to Elysium before I allow that to happen," Arenius growled through clenched teeth, his knuckles turning white as he tightly grasped the swords handle.

"I plan to," the Praetorian whispered, allowing the winds to fall silent.

Arenius stood like a statue, absorbing the eerie symphony of the gentle wind and the snapping flames, his resolve steeling against the notion of surrendering to death. The mere thought sent a shiver down his spine, knowing that if he perished, so too would his parents, unless fate had already claimed them. With a deep breath, he shut his eyes, clearing his mind as he anticipated the imminent attack from his foe.

With his senses honing, he sensed their presence in the shadows, a cautious step followed by two more, each footfall snapping twigs and rustling dry leaves under the Praetorians' boots. The sound drew nearer, echoing through the eerie stillness of the night.

Following Cornelius's rigorous training, Arenius regulated his breath, each inhale and exhale measured. He honed in on the subtle sounds around him, the rustle of leaves overhead, the distant chirping of crickets. His muscles tensed with anticipation as he waited for his opponent's move. With precision born from countless hours of practice, he shifted his weight subtly, angling himself to create an opportune moment to launch a decisive attack.

The battle is not over until your enemy is on the ground, breath no longer entering his body, Arenius replayed his father's words in his mind.

Suddenly, the sixth and final step materialized before him, appearing as if from thin air.

Arenius dropped to one knee, his blade slicing through the air with a swift motion, but it found nothing but emptiness. The rush of wind brushed past him as he anticipated an attack that never materialized. Swift on his feet, the praetorian altered his course at the final instant, causing him to skid and stumble towards the roaring flames. As he crashed into the fiery inferno, his body convulsed and roared in agony, fiery sparks clinging to his searing flesh. With urgency in his movements, the guard frantically swatted away the burning debris that clung to him.

Capitalizing on the moment, Arenius charged towards his assailant, brandishing his sword menacingly. As they closed in on each other, he brought his blade down upon his adversary.

Clank.

Arenius' eyes widened seeing the blade blocked mid-air by the Praetorian's wrist guard.

"Do you think that's all it takes to rid yourself of me?" the guard hissed, slowly moving Arenius' blade aside.

Arenius had little time to react before the giant Praetorian grabbed him by the collar and leg, hoisting him over his head. In an instant the ground was rushing towards him as he was slammed into the dirt with such force which would have otherwise crushed the bones of another. Dirt exploded upwards, swallowing him as he sank six inches into the earth.

Buried several inches in the soil, a plume of dirt settling around him, the Praetorian paced in front the fire. Its fiery glow reflecting off his armor and iron sword, adding to his demonic nature.

Staring Arenius down though he was a wounded prey, "You like playing with swords, I see," taking a moment to observe the glowing blade in Arenius' hand. Then pulled free the sword at his side, the sharp sound of metal scrapping metal filling. "How about we have ourselves a friendly spar?"

Rising from the dirt, Arenius was promptly reminded, how being a Vir did not dull his sense of pain in the slightest. If anything, they were heightened. However, if he wished to survive and see his parents again, thoughts of pain had to be pushed aside. He could not bring himself to image what life would be like without them, and would he be able to continue on?

How could I allow being a Vir, overshadow their safety? What kind of a son am I?

Grimacing under the pain, Arenius lifted his blade into a thrusting position.

"That's the spirit," the Praetorian smiled, squaring into combat stance, holding the sword with two hands out in front of him.

For several moments neither moved, waiting for the other. Until Arenius dashed forward with a perfect thrust, covering the nine-foot gap in seconds. The Praetorian guard was surprised by such a prompt attack from a young boy, but he did not become one of Augustus' close guards to be taken out by a single strike.

Keeping a strong stance, he parried Arenius' first attack. Yet it was quickly followed up with a second, third and fourth. Having such power and force put behind each parry and strike, sparks flew in every direction as the two blades collided. Staggering back, but managing to stay on his feet, the Praetorian easily regained his balanced, and continued to parry the flurry of attacks.

"That's it," laughed the giant, shoving Arenius back with his last attack. "Now it's my turn."

The Praetorian zipped forward swinging at Arenius using all his strength, blocking with his sword, the blow sent him soaring backwards, away from the safety of the camp's light, and into the dark forest. While Arenius was in flight and before hitting the dirt, the Praetorian shoulder charged, sending Arenius sailing sideways. Crashing through trees, he hit the dirt tumbling end over end, to come to a halt at the base of a tree several feet away. He had little time to gather or scan himself for injuries before a decaying tree trunk came hurling from above. At the last second, the tree slammed into the ground where he stood moments ago.

"You're out of your element on this one, Vir," a voice growled from the dark forest's canopy.

Arenius eyes darted sporadically from side to side while trying to lock on to the rustling trees above. His opponent freely dashed amongst the tree branches, causing loose leaves to descend like fallen feathers. Using the glow from his sword to illuminate the surrounding dark, the large Praetorian descended from the trees, his blade held over head ready to strike. Arenius rolled to the side allowing the Praetorian's blade to slice through the fallen tree decayed with little effort. Emerging from his roll, Arenius instantly thrusted his blade through his attacker's thigh. He expected to guard to cry out in pain, yet there was nothing. The only evidence he had of striking his target, was the blood dripping from his blade.

Grabbing both Arenius' hand and blade guard, the Praetorian eased the sword from his leg. Lifting Arenius so they were face to face, "This body is only a shell, destroy it and I'll get a better one," he smirked, before tossing Arenius like a useless stick across the forest floor.

Arenius rolled once before stabbing his gladius in the dirt, the divinium blade carved a long line in the earth until it brought him to a sliding stop. "No matter how many soldiers you bring before me, they will all fall beneath my blade, until I find my parents!"

Giving his best war cry, Arenius dashed forward with a fury of strikes. The first was swung at the Praetorian's neck, leaning back he narrowly dodged the attack, allowing the blade to pass inches from the throat. Keeping up the offensive, Arenius pulled the blade upward, slashing the Praetorian across his armored breastplate, parting the well-crafted material as though it was common grass. Desperate to defend himself and feeling the burn along their chest as Arenius blade had not only cut through their armor but down to their flesh as well. The Praetorian countered and began unleashing his own attacks which Arenius easily evaded with slides and spins. Having his opponent flustered was exactly what he needed, and with each blow Arenius' sword chipped more and more steel from the Praetorians sword. With one final blow he shattered the praetorians weapon into many flickering pierces as his sword proceeded to at the guard's knees, slicing through bone.

The giant man growled in pain while collapsing under his weight. Before the praetorian hit the ground, Arenius was already in the air, bringing his weapon down with all his strength behind him. *"Never give your enemy time to recover,"* he could hear Cornelius saying to him, as the tip of the blade penetrated the soldier's face and out the back of his helmet, pinning his head to the dirt.

Arenius gripped his weapon tightly, crouching next to the Praetorian's convulsing form. The Praetorian's body shimmered with a blinding light, disintegrating before his eyes. As the radiant display faded, Arenius fought to steady his ragged breaths, the once-glowing sword now dimmed, casting him back into a realm of shadows.

X

Cornelius and Floriana stirred from their slumber, feeling the haze of artificial sleep lingering in their minds. As they regained consciousness, they realized their mouths were muffled by linen and their heads covered with a burlap bag infused with the pungent scent of garlic. Laying with their backs to each other, their wrists secured behind their backs, they bounced along the uneven path, finding solace in intertwining their fingers to soothe their nerves of the unknown. Cornelius felt the familiar warmth of Floriana's touch, his grip on her hands growing firmer to steady her trembling, not out of fear, but from the overwhelming sense of being ensnared.

He knew Floriana's fearless demeanor never wavered, except when it came to the overwhelming dread of a mother contemplating the possibility of losing her son. Should their lives end tonight, he couldn't imagine sharing his final moments with anyone else. Despite contemplating the possibility of death, his mind kept drifting to Arenius's whereabouts and well-being. Before redirecting his thoughts to their immediate predicament: devising an escape plan.

With his head covered, it was impossible for Cornelius to keep track of the direction they had been traveling for the last hour. Not long after waking up did, he identified the bumpy carriage they were being transported in, from the clanking merchant items he had no doubt they belonged to Cecelia. The biggest mystery lay in the group of men following closely on horseback.

Who were they, what did they want, and what did they do with Cecelia and Arenius? Whatever their intent maybe, it could not be good.

Due to the carriage's constant *squeaks* and *clanks*, drowning out their sounds of the world he had abandoned any attempts to listen in. At the moment he had to accept, he was a prisoner along with his wife and thoughts.

The carriage rumbled along a neglected dirt trail, its sides brushed by overgrown grass and weeds that seemed untouched for years. At the trail's conclusion, Praetorian guards stood sentinel in front of an abandoned villa. The villa, once grand with two imposing Corinthian columns at its entrance, now stood as a shadow of its former glory. Vines enveloped the structure, claiming it as their own and painting a picture of decay and neglect.

"Finally," grumbled a Praetorian soldier as he briskly approached, seizing the horse's reins and secured the carriage to a sturdy post. With practiced efficiency, he then tended to the captive's trio of horses tethered at the back of the carriage.

"I got here as fast as I could. If..."

The soldier promptly raised a hand, cutting off Cecelia, "Save it for Augustus. He'll want to deal with you himself."

"*So, she is here,*" Cornelius thought upon hearing her name, all the while still tied in the carriage.

Trepidation gripped Cecelia as Augustus' name echoed, silencing her instantly. She remained silent while the two guards moved toward the back of the carriage. With a swift motion, they unveiled a concealed cloth covering, revealing Floriana and

Cornelius bound amidst the assortment of goods belonging to the merchant.

"I believe this is going to be our promotion," The second guard grinned as he reached out for the thick, rough ropes tightly coiled around Floriana's slender ankles.

Coarse fingers grazed her skin, prompting an instinctive flurry of movement as she fiercely writhed against the intrusion, her muffled protests lost beneath the tight gag.

"Oh, she is fiery. Don't worry, beautiful, it will be over soon," He joked, playfully drawing her closer, smoothly lifting her onto his shoulder as if she were a child.

"What are you waiting for? Get inside and do what you are here to do," Soldier one's voice sliced through the air, sharp and commanding. "You think things are going to prepare themselves? Get to work! Your no longer needed out here," the ended, shoeing her away.

Lowering her head, Cecelia obeyed the commands given to her and began descending the carriage. Being sure to grab a few items from the carriage, before scurrying away into the ruined home.

Following the intense battle with the colossal praetorian, Arenius embarked on a desperate quest to locate his parents. Overwhelmed by fear and uncertainty, he grappled with the unfamiliar sensation of being lost in a world fraught with danger. Amidst the chaos, a realization dawned on him – every lesson his father had imparted unknowingly equipped him for this very moment.

"I should have pushed myself harder during training. If I did, I

would know exactly what to do," he thought to himself, pacing near the fire.

"How could you let them take them?" Collapsing to knees, burying his head in his palm, "You fool, so focused on yourself," he argued with himself, tears rolling down his face.

Looking to the sky flames flickering on his face, "Why them and not me?"

With his knees buried in the dirt, he listened to the crackling wood, when a twig snapped just beyond the light's threshold. Arenius made subtle movements as his hand reached out for his weapon. He could sense something weighty approaching behind him.

"Not another one already," he thought.

Right on his heels, a presence lingered. Gripping the gladius tightly, he swiftly pivoted, unsheathing his sword in one fluid motion, poised for combat. Instead of a warrior or a fiend, a buck stood before him, its gaze inquisitive. Arenius sheathed his weapon cautiously, so as not to alarm the creature.

After a moment of neither of them moving, the buck majestically began to drew near, its crowned antlers bobbed up and down. Arenius extended his hand out as it cautiously sniffed it before continuing on its journey past him. Keeping his hand extended, allowing him to brush across the deer's smooth fur which burned red in the flames light. With every breath the beast took, he could feel the beast immense strength.

His gaze remained fixed on the deer, its eyes meeting his briefly before it gracefully slipped out of view, vanishing into the dense embrace of the forest.

"I understand," he muttered, wiping away what tears remained.

Following Cornelius's teachings, he honed in on his breath,

aligning his thoughts and physical being, a serene energy enveloping him. A novel sensation washed over him, akin to a gentle push from an unseen hand. Uncertain of the purpose but driven by an inexplicable impulse, he stood up. Surveying the surroundings, his gaze swept across the landscape, seeking any trace that might unveil the whereabouts of his missing parents. However, all that met his eyes was emptiness; the blankets, steeds, and crackling fire.

"What do they want with my parents," he thought, standing to his feet, rushing into the forest for a sturdy branch.

Having the branch in hand, he tore several stripes from his clothing and tied them to the top of the branch. Igniting the fabric, he search the area. It did not take long for his eyes to fall on what he was looking for; carriage tracks leading away from camp and out of the stone pine Forest. Tightly clutching the hilt of his sheath, he sprinted off, following the tracks.

Guided by the mysterious force propelling his senses, he pushed himself as hard as he could, he focused on planting one foot in front of the other.

After being unceremoniously thrown onto the chilly tiles of the old villa, Cornelius and Floriana found themselves abandoned by the soldiers who departed to resume their patrol, leaving Cecelia to attend to her tasks. Despite the barrier of the bag over his head, Cornelius couldn't escape the musty scent that pervaded the room, a mixture of dampness and blood that reminded him of countless prison garrisons he had encountered in his military campaigns. He had come to recognize that the combination of blood and dampness always signified impending trouble.

Peering through the woven fibers of the sack, they observed a silhouette gliding across the chamber, unmistakably Cecelia with her deliberate, hushed footfalls. Shedding her cloak, she drew nearer to Cornelius and Floriana, unveiling their faces. The harsh glare from numerous oil lamps caused discomfort to their eyes, yet most of the illumination in the space emanated from the flickering hearth in the kitchen.

With the bags off, it revealed a scene that captured their attention immediately. Seated in the corner of what appeared to be a dilapidated kitchen, they noticed its ancient charm. The ceiling showed signs of decay with parts of it caved in, creating an opening for plants to grow through, cascading down the wall in a mix of green and brown hues. Their gaze then landed on the focal point of the room – a table equipped with sturdy iron shackles for wrists and ankles.

"Shush," Cecelia motioned with a finger held to her mouth, "It's probably not wise for me to be talking to you, so keep your voices down," Cecelia whispered, glancing over her shoulders, ensuring they were alone before removing the gag from their mouths.

Being untied first, "What's this about? What do you want with us? Where are we?" Floriana barked, her eyes burning with fury.

"Quiet please," she insisted, checking the entrances again. "I cannot share our location and it's not you that they want," Cecelia answered, untying Cornelius' gag. "It's him," gesturing to Cornelius "and your son they were after," stepping away to continue her job.

"Where is my son?" Cornelius asked, doing his best to remain calm.

"That, I'm unsure of. He was ordered to be left behind. If Augustus had his way, I'm sorry to say, he is most likely no longer among the living," she paused, a brief moment of sympathy shown on her face, then walked to the trough to dice vegetables.

Cornelius struggled to sit himself up against the wall, "Well, what does Augustus want with me?"

"Isn't it obvious, dear General? Augustus wants you on his side, for he is soon to take control of the Republic as his own. And he wants strong dedicated soldiers like yourself as his pawns. To be his Daemones possessed Praetorian Guard to execute his very bidding," she stated, tossing diced vegetables in the boiling pot.

"I would never serve him again!" Cornelius said through clenched teeth.

"Many others have spoken those same words, General. I myself being one of them. But believe me, he has ways to break even the strongest will. First, he has demons which will watch your every move, then by spilling your blood. And if that doesn't motivate you, he spills the blood of those you love," her voice cracking with emotion, as she glanced at Floriana.

"I would never allow that to happen," Cornelius growled.

"You already have, General. You already have," she said, returning to her task her back towards them. "Augustus has become too powerful and there's nothing commoners like ourselves can do to stop him."

"How could you do this to us? We helped you when no one else was around?" Floriana pleaded.

"Everything you thought you were doing was all planned by Augustus. He already knows what you think you know. The demons are very clever and knew you would be passing through at some point, so they had me mislead you into thinking I was some helpless old lady. And for that I'm truly sorry," Cecelia explained, not taking her eyes from stirring a pot on the trough.

"Why can't you stop cooking and just look at us? Who are you cooking for? We for sure are not going to take anything from you." Floriana snapped, her voice echoing in the isolated house.

"*Shh*, I warned you to keep it down. And you should heed my words, if you knew what was good for you," she whispered, rushing over to them, in an attempt to calm him. "This meal is not for you, but you will be helping with it," Cecelia said, then began her way back to the pot.

"What is that supposed to mean?" Floriana pushed back, getting Cecelia to stop in her tracks.

"Unfortunately, for you, Floriana, it means you're of no use to them like your husband. The soldiers who caught you, enjoy having their prisoners fresh," she said, gesturing to the blood-stained table with wrist and ankle irons.

"You're not saying, they intend on eating her," Cornelius questioned.

Cecelia paused, as though she was considering the facts, "That's exactly what I'm saying. Not all Daemones fancy the taste of humans, but a small group view us as a delicacy."

Those words sent a wave of nausea through Floriana's stomach. The idea of becoming someone's meal churned her insides, making her concentrate hard on holding back the meager food she had consumed.

Cornelius scooted himself closer, "Cecelia, you can't let them do this to us. We are not the enemy."

"I am aware of this, but there is, as I said before, little I can do to help. And, I'm sorry."

Allowing an uncanny sense to guide him where he needed to be, Arenius made his way through the high brush, that cloaked the villa from prying eyes on the road. Kneeling, Arenius partially pulled his gladius from its sheath, to find exactly what he felt. His blade was glowing deeply with its color; thus, demons were nearby. Under the darkness of cover, he did a quick study of his injuries and found his cuts had almost healed and bruises all but gone. He could not help but to think being a Vir was weird and fantastic at the same time.

His lithe build proved advantageous, enabling him to slink undetected through the shadows. Concealed amidst the dense foliage, Arenius spied two soldiers meandering along the perimeter of the mansion. He fixed his gaze on them as they conversed nonchalantly, their movements betraying no hint of the malevolent entities lurking within them.

The villa stood grandly before him, its once pristine plaster now weathered and chipped, revealing the sturdy brick beneath. Though not as spacious as their luxurious domus in the countryside, it still offered ample room. The sight of smoke spiraling from the chimney drew his gaze, hinting at the presence of others seeking shelter for the night. This unexpected discovery sparked a glimmer of hope within him - perhaps his parents had managed to survive against all odds.

His immediate impulse pushed him to launch an attack during their vulnerable moment, yet a nagging feeling deep within him advised against it. He understood that a direct assault might draw attention and endanger his parents if additional soldiers lurked inside. Left with no alternative, he decided to bide his time until the two dispersed or became less vigilant, allowing him to level the playing field.

Arenius bided his time hidden in the lush grass as the Praetorian Guards finally ceased their chatter and dispersed for their patrols. Seizing the opportunity he had been patiently waiting for, one guard stationed himself to watch over the weed-covered path towards the road, while the other soldier began to move stealthily around its perimeter towards the back.

As the lead soldier swiveled, his back now an open invitation, Arenius seized his chance. With a swift and soundless departure from the sanctuary of the bushes, he traversed a distance that would take a regular man several heartbeats in just one. In one smooth motion he unsheathed his divinium gladius and held it tight within his grasp.

Like a phantom, he closed in on the unsuspecting guard from behind. His hand clamped over the soldier's mouth, muffling any potential cries for help even before they were formed. Then, with a surge of power guided by precision, he drove his blade into the gap between the soldier's shoulders.

The divinium gladius bit through armor as though it was mere cloth and emerged victorious on the other side through the breastplate. It left in its wake a path of destruction within the guard's body. Arenius bore the weight of his dying adversary until there was no more life to snuff out, until every vestige of demonic presence had been banished back to the Nether.

Swiftly, he melted back into the obscurity of the shadows, leaving the lifeless form of the first soldier to evaporated into nothingness. He then tread lightly along the exact trail that had been imprinted by the boots of the second soldier just moments before. As he neared the corner of the dilapidated house, he cautiously leaned to get a glimpse around it. There, unaware and vulnerable, was his target. The soldier was idly nudging rocks and rubble with his boot in a rhythm born out of sheer boredom, utterly oblivious to the imminent threat that was stealthily closing in on him.

Before the soldier's gaze could shift to the radiant blade amidst the shadows, Arenius materialized, brandishing his gladius high above. Swift as a striking viper, he flung the weapon towards the soldier. The gladius transformed into a shimmering violet disk mid-flight, piercing through the air with lethal precision until it lodged deep in the soldier's chest. In seconds, the Praetorian's form started disintegrating into ethereal sparks, dissipating into the nocturnal breeze.

In a swift motion, the blade plummeted from above, its descent culminating in a solid thump as it met the grass below. Arenius paused briefly to catch his breath before he stooped to retrieve his sword. Determination etched on his face, he ascended onto the rooftop, driven by the curiosity to peer through and witness the unfolding events within.

"Do you think I chose this for my life, to forever be their slave? A bond between demons and humans is not something easily broken," Cecelia argued, Stirring the pot vigorously as though it would ease her pain. Stirring the pot vigorously, Cecelia engaged in a heated debate. Her back remained turned to them, her shoulders visibly trembling as she struggled to hold back tears.

"Bond? What are you talking about, lady?" Cornelius barked back.

Facing them, Cecelia drew in a long breath, her chest rising and falling with the intake of air as she prepared to speak. "You don't understand, for those who don't willingly submit themselves into servitude. Daemons are very determined and can find other ways to convince their will. This is not how I wished my life to be. My husband refused to help their cause. And afterward I was forced to watch them torture him until his body could no longer endure. May the gods grant him place in the Elysian fields," tears streaming down her face. "Although my son no longer lived with us, they somehow knew of him. Warning me, that if I did not aid them when needed, then he and his family would suffer in my husband's misfortunes," wiping her tears away. "Children should not journey to the next life before their parents," she whispered.

Despite being bound and facing the looming threat of being devoured, Floriana's heart momentarily fluttered before the harsh reality crashed back in, "How can you say that with such ease, when you just gave our son to them? Which is on top of, threatening to feed us to them. How are you any different from the Daemones?"

"I would do anything for my son like you," Cecelia's voice erupted like a thunderclap, the wooden spoon in her hand jabbing the air with each word she emphasized, "They know things! Things there shouldn't be knowledge of. Torturous things," her voice softening. "No matter where I'm at they find me, and know of my doings. Once I agreed, I was no longer capable of saying no. How can I combat such forces? To this day, my son does not know how his father really died. My secrecy and servitude keeps him and his family alive and that's worth it."

"Is the cost of this worth the lives of others?" Floriana's voice echoed through the room.

"If it means-," Cecelia halts mid-sentence, her words abruptly silenced by the abrupt impact of a heavy thud echoing through the room behind her.

Startled by the noise, she pivoted around to see Arenius illuminated by the moonlight peeking through the rubble above, his grip firm on the gladius in his hand.

"Y-You," she stammered.

"Arenius, you're alive," Floriana greeted, tears of joy streaming from her eyes.

"Striker her down, Arenius," Cornelius ordered.

Fear gripped Cecelia's heart, her breath quickening as Arenius advanced towards her, the glint of his gladius catching the dim light. "I'd understand if you killed me. I would do the same to protect those I love," backing away cautiously, she retreated until the cold touch of the wall met her spine.

Centered on Cecelia, Arenius lifted his weapon high above his head. Left with no alternative, Cecelia shut her eyes, yearning that when she dared to look again, she would find herself reunited with her husband. But that moment never arrived. Instead of the sharp swish of a blade cutting through the air, she was met with the distinct sound of Arenius securely returning his weapon to its sheath. Soon after, a gentle hand tenderly rested on her forehead, offering solace in the midst of uncertainty.

"*Foeda noxreditum ad Nethera*," Arenius began to chant, causing a small light to emit from his palm, "*Foeda noxreditum ad Nethera* (Foul of the night, return to the Nether)."

Every syllable spoken heightened the brightness in the room, until it radiantly illuminated the previously shadowy space, compelling Cornelius and Floriana to shield their eyes.

A blazing emblem appeared on her neck, as if burned by a searing brand, catching Arenius's attention. It bore an unfamiliar design, yet its significance resonated with him. While he recited his incantations, the circular symbol with a serpent-like line at its core gradually dissolved, leaving her skin restored to its original state.

Fear gripped Cecelia, its icy fingers slowly thawing as a radiant smile spread across her face, infusing her with a warmth she hadn't felt in years. As she exhaled, all the burdens that had weighed her down seemed to dissolve into nothingness. Gradually opening her eyes, she was met with the towering calm presence of Arenius.

Cecelia's smile widened, a glint of newfound liberation in her eyes. "His gaze no longer lingers on me," she whispered, a sense of wonder coloring her words. "I feel unshackled. How can this be real?"

Arenius calmly looked into her eyes, "Now go, reach your son before the Daemones do."

"What, how can I repay you for this?" Cecelia asked.

"No payment needed. You gave so much in your life already. Now go!"

"Gratitude," she murmured, sidestepping him, her gaze briefly touching upon Cornelius and Floriana bound in the shadows, "Regrets weigh heavy on me for my actions." With a parting glance before heading towards her waiting carriage, she added softly, "Your purse rests by the trough," then vanished from view.

"What do you think you are doing?" Cornelius barked. "She could give our location away!"

"She won't," Arenius exclaimed calmly, making his way over and cutting them free of their bonds.

"How can you be sure?" Hurrying to catch up with Cecelia, Cornelius felt a strong grip on his wrist as Arenius pulled him back, his eyes filled with concern.

"I can sense it. She's liberated in some way. From what exactly? I cannot pinpoint. It felt as though the Daemones had ensnared her mind with an invisible chain, linking her to their desires and commands. Yet, that bond has been shattered," Arenius declared, his grip firm as Cornelius struggled to break free. "Father, release her, I beg of you. She is no longer under their control."

Cornelius strained against Arenius' grasp once more, only to recognize the unyielding strength of his teenage son's grip.

"Please, Pa," Arenius pleaded.

"Fine," he relented, giving up the pursuit to help Florianna to her feet.

"We thought you were dead," Florianna said, giving him a hug, immediately checking him for injuries. "We thought we lost you son!"

"I'm alright," he reassured her while she persisted in examining him. "Mom, really, I'm okay," he insisted, gently taking hold of her hands to halt her actions. "I promise, I'm perfectly fine!"

"I see," Floriana said, calming herself. And sensing the change in Arenius, who in a short number of days, was no longer the same teenager who had started this journey. "How did you find us? And what was that whole thing with Cecelia?" Looking at the door she had exited.

"All this is new to me as well. It's like I knew, an uncanny knowing where to go and when I got here, what Cecelia needed. I listened to her talk to you about her family and her bond to the Daemones from the roof, when images from the past began to flood my memory. They were part of me, as though I share all the basic skills and knowledge of all who possessed the stone before me. The same thing happened when I had to fight a demon in the forest, after both of you were taken. I believe the stone has the power to break the bonds demons have on the unfortunate people they happen to control. When they accept demons, they have to do their bidding. Even if they know them to be wrong. They're just pawns," Arenius ended, glancing down at his hands.

Floriana and Cornelius exchanged looks, "Whatever all this

is, we are here for you," Floriana said, breaking the odd silence before once again taking him in her embrace. "Right Cornelius," cutting him a glance.

"Right," Cornelius agreed, standing at the room's door. "We have to get moving, it's not safe here."

"Cornelius!" Florianna shouted.

Taking a deep breath, Cornelius walks over to the two of them and places a firm hand on Arenius' shoulder, "Good job, son. There's no telling what they would have done if you hadn't arrived."

"Thanks, Pa."

"Well, I think we've all had enough rest this night. Grab whatever you need and let's get out of here. We need to reach Ostia before anything else happens."

All were in accord as Cornelius carefully fastened the jingling coin pouch to his belt, Floriana gathered up the last scraps of food provisions, and Arenius briskly left the villa to ready the horses for their imminent journey.

XI

Several years had passed since Floriana last stepped foot in Ostia, a vibrant city known for its bustling trade, lively taverns, and enticing brothels. As she gazed upon the familiar sights, it was as if time stood still. Memories flooded back of the day Cornelius embarked from Ostia alongside Octavian to quell the rebellion of Mark Anthony and Queen Cleopatra. The essence of the city remained unchanged – the stretching wooden docks at the harbor's edge, the rows of brick residences reaching towards the sky, and the enthusiastic vendors crowding the market square, eager to engage any passerby.

The sight of the bustling crowds caught her off guard. While not as densely packed as the throngs in Rome, it resembled a smaller counterpart to the grand city. She suspected its new-found affluence stemmed from the empire's absorption of the opulent realm of Egypt and its lands, fueling the urban center's economic growth and development. Noteworthy among its attributes was the expansive and regal harbor, serving not only as a shield against ocean swells but also warding off pirate threats effectively.

Strolling along the bustling streets cloaked in a hood, Floriana observed the array of vendors selling familiar goods from Rome, but at more affordable prices. Assigned by Cornelius to procure supplies for their journey, she discreetly carried a sword by her side. Meanwhile, Cornelius and Arenius hustled to secure passage on the next departing vessel from the mainland.

Under the warm glow of the evening sun, she meandered through a variety of objects, envisioning how each could enhance their living space. Among them, her gaze lingered on a collection of oversized amphora jars designed for storing wine. A smile played on her lips as she recalled Cornelius' excitement about potentially establishing a vineyard once his term of service was fulfilled. Through these daydreams of an alternate reality, she found solace in momentarily escaping the harsh reality that everything she had painstakingly built had been mercilessly dismantled in just one fateful night.

"Why my family, why my son," she though, bringing herself back to reality.

Cornelius and she had often conversed about scenarios such as these: his absence after a military expedition, a rival kingdom advancing towards their city, or internal strife shaking the government and displacing their household. While these possibilities were tangible, she had never truly envisioned experiencing them firsthand. Yet, that day had dawned upon her life, not due to conflict or scarcity, but because her son had emerged as a Vir, a legendary figure fated to bring aid to the world.

Questions raced through her mind: Could her family ever return to their previous life, or was survival itself uncertain? How would she navigate such a daunting challenge?

Any other wife's family would likely have surrendered by now, but the Vesta lineage was far from ordinary. With the indomitable spirit of Spartans coursing through her blood, she was destined for resilience.

Floriana brushed away those concerns to concentrate on the current objective of procuring additional provisions, despite each ship they sailed on being stocked with sufficient supplies for everyone aboard. In contrast to Rome's winding and intricate pathways, she adeptly maneuvered through Ostia's organized grid streets to procure the necessary supplies.

Completing her checklist by buying a few slices of savory salted pork and crusty sourdough bread for their trio, she paused at a stall to appreciate the intricate arrangement of shimmering jewelry on display.

"How much for this one?" she asked the vendor, selecting a delicate bracelet crafted from tiny sea shells adorned with intricate patterns of shimmering purples and blues.

A wiry man in his forties sprang up from his market stall, bearing the weathered look of one accustomed to toiling under the sun. "That's two *assarrii*," he replied.

"That's pricey for some simple shells, don't you think?" Floriana asked.

"Well, considering these shells come from distant lands, far from here, I don't think so," his warm hazel eyes crinkled at the corners, exuding a sense of comfort as she meticulously examined the object in front of her.

"And what lands would that be?" she questioned, giving him a puzzling stare.

The gruff man paused to gather his thoughts, "*Ah*, I remember now, that would be the shores of Miletus."

"Are they now?" she smiled, admiring the shell's deep and rich colors. She found the bracelet to be beautiful no matter its origins, as it reminded her of the coast from her homeland.

As the vendor enthusiastically rambled on about the exquisite craftsmanship of his shell bracelets, Floriana felt a prickling sensation on her neck. A sense of unease crept over her, making her feel as if a multitude of eyes were fixated on her. Swiftly, she pivoted and scrutinized the bustling crowd, her gaze flitting rapidly through the sea of faces in search of anything out of the ordinary.

Midway through stirring her pan, she caught sight of a solitary Roman soldier, donned in the dark armor reminiscent of the guards at Mercury's temple, fixedly observing her from the opposite end of the bustling market square. The throng of people milling about obstructed a clear view of his countenance, his helmet casting shadows over his features. Despite the shielded gaze behind the visor, an unsettling feeling crept over her that he was delving into the depths of her being. Even in his immobility, an undeniable sense lingered that his intentions towards her were malicious in nature.

In a sudden flutter of movement, the soldier disappeared into the bustling crowd. Left alone, she lingered, scanning each passing face in search of any trace of the enigmatic figure who had just vanished.

"How could a soldier clad in gleaming armor, disappear without a trace," she pondered. Yet, vanish he did, leaving behind nothing but an eerie emptiness.

"If you're not going to buy, please place it down and step to the side. You're blocking others from seeing," the vendor insisted, bringing Floriana back to her senses.

"Sorry," facing the man. "Here you go," handing him a silver *denarius* with the likeness of Julius Caesar stamped on its sides.

"This is too much," the man said, confused at the amount she had given him. "This is more than triple what it cost lady."

"Don't worry about it, keep it," she insisted.

The man's face lit up, "Thank you. Do come back," the

merchant replied, taking the money.

Swiftly tucking the bracelet into her leather shoulder bag, she scanned the bustling crowd one final time. With a determined stride, she navigated through the throng of people, making her way towards the labyrinthine paths leading to the busy shipping docks.

The vibrant metropolis of Ostia thrived due to a bustling port that never seemed to rest. From the crack of dawn until dusk, an array of vessels crowded the numerous docks, with additional ships bobbing in the harbor, eager to offload their precious cargo. These piers became a hive of activity as mighty fleets discharged their valuable grain harvested from the fertile lands of Sardinia and Sicily. Smaller, more nimble boats arrived laden with amphorae filled with exquisite wines and aromatic oils.

Arenius and Cornelius made their way towards the hectic dock, where a mix of laborers and slaves hurried back and forth under the weight of crates and barrels. The workers transported goods from the arriving merchant ships to the government warehouses that stood along the water's edge, as well as to various stalls in the vibrant market square.

"Are you sure it was safe to send mom alone?" Arenius asked, as they meandered through the streets.

"Your mother," Cornelius went to respond, then lowered his voice. "Your mother is capable of being on her own. If you want to worry about something, you need to worry if Augustus' order for our arrest reached every city from her to Egypt," his eyes cautiously monitoring the movements of others. "Besides, splitting up allows us to accomplish things quicker."

"Is that really all you have to say, considering what happened last night? Who knows, they could still be out there searching for us, and Ma is out there alone," Arenius pressed on, halting abruptly in the midst of the deserted road.

"Don't you think I know that?" Cornelius stressed, taking hold of Arenius' arm, leading him aside.

"How would I know? From what I've seen you only make choices that's best for you," Arenius argued.

"You wouldn't have an inkling of what it means to make choices, especially with your mother carrying you every step," Cornelius barked with a whisper, his eyes like darts staring into Arenius. Gathering his composure, he checked to make sure he was not overheard, "Right now is not the time for this. The faster we get what we need, the faster we get out of here. Your mother is grabbing a few supplies while we handle the dock master and get passage aboard a ship bound for Tarsus. So, I advise you to fall in and-,"

"And what, be a good soldier?" Arenius said, watching his father's face turn red as the sitting sun.

Inhaling deeply, "Just fall in," Cornelius ended, before strolling towards the closest dock.

"Be a good little soldier and full in," Arenius mocked with a whisper, shaking his head, he falls in behind Cornelius.

Strolling down the pier, Cornelius caught sight of his target - the Harbor Master. Engaged in his duties, as they meticulously inspected each ship with a wax tablet clutched in his hand.

"That's him," Cornelius whispered urgently, halting abruptly, Arenius close beside him. "Stay back and let me handle this."

"Why? I can handle myself," Arenius defended.

"That's not it. I need to go alone, in case word has reached the ports about us. If I'm captured, I need you to find your mother and leave the city immediately."

Feeling a wave of uncertainty washing over him, Arenius found himself grappling with the daunting prospect of navigating life's challenges without his father by his side. As he pondered this new reality, he couldn't help but wonder how he would cope without his father's guidance. Cornelius's absence sparked a flurry of unanticipated scenarios in Arenius's mind, making him realize the profound impact his father had on both his sorrows and triumphs throughout the years.

"Arenius, do you understand me?"

"Yes, I understand," Arenius replied.

"Good. And keep your eyes open for anything out of the ordinary," Cornelius added, patting him on the shoulder.

With limited choices, Arenius observed from a distance as his father made his way towards the Harbormaster, easily distinguishable in the non-stop crowd. Their vibrant tunic, adorned with intricate patterns and draping gracefully over his slender figure, unmistakably signified his high rank. Despite the ambiguity of his origins, the Harbormaster's gestures and rich skin tone hinted at a heritage beyond Roman descent. Flanking him were two slaves, positioned on either side, each holding up a linen canopy supported by long poles to shield him from the relentless Mediterranean sun.

Cornelius was welcomed with a warm embrace and a wide smile. Engaging in a lengthy discussion, he would intermittently glance at Arenius to ensure his companion stayed in place. As their conversation drew to a close, Cornelius retrieved the leather pouch hidden beneath his cloak and passed it over to the Harbormaster, who accepted it with evident delight. After a final exchange of words, Cornelius took his leave.

"We've secured passage to Tarsus," Cornelius shared, returning to Arenius. "The Adresta departs at sundown. We now need to find your mother," he said, promptly leading Arenius away from the pier to a location behind one of the storage buildings, and away from peering eyes.

"I'm not sure Tarsus is where we should go," Arenius said hesitantly.

Uncertain as to what he was alluding to, Cornelius stepped, well within Arenius' comfort zone. "No, no. You will not do this now. The decision has been made, Tarsus is our home now," he declared through clenched teeth.

"That may not be what's best," Arenius insisted.

"What's best? Let's talk about what you believe is best. We already did two things you believed to be best. Both of which I disagreed with. First, helping the old lady, and secondly, letting her go. Which I hope doesn't hurt us in return. Just keep to yourself what you believe to be best."

"Pa, that doesn't change a thing," Arenius continued, being cautious of his volume and tone, "We can't kill everyone. And I let her go because her bond with the demons was broken."

"Why not, if it means us surviving another day? The world doesn't act kind to those unwilling to get things done! But you with your vast experience would understand how that works. Listen here, keeping her alive may have endangered us ten times over. Augustus will be sure to have soldiers on our trail."

"Are you suggesting we commit a ruthless murder? To take the life of an elderly woman who was simply defending her son?" Arenius exclaimed, his tone growing more intense.

"Exactly," Cornelius replied, his face a mask of indifference.

Stunned by his father's words, Arenius took several steps back. *"How can he kill in cold blood?"* He thought.

Frustrated, he flung his hands up in the air. "Enough of

this. We must locate your mother and get ready for departure," he declared before striding off, assuming Arenius would come along.

"But-"

"Enough, Arenius," Cornelius shot, cutting Arenius' words short.

"Look at you, taking off again. Never considering how I feel," Arenius continued.

"What was that?" he stopped, returning to Arenius.

"If you're heading for Tarsus, I'm not coming," Arenius insisted, standing his ground.

"You'll go where I tell you to go," Cornelius added, towering over Arenius.

"Not today, and you know there's nothing you can do to make me. Not anymore. I've dreamed of the day that I would be able to go on one of your journeys. But things are different now," he stated, exhaling deeply. "I need to go to Alexandria."

"Alexandria! What's in Alexandria?" Cornelius questioned, pacing a short distance.

"I just need to."

"You may not know this because you have never left the mainland. But Alexandria is a province of Rome. It belongs to Rome. Everywhere you think you can go, now belongs to Rome. And if you're wondering how I know, it's because I helped take it."

"All I know is when we were at camp in the stone pine forest, I saw it, in a vision. It was as clear as you standing before me. And I heard the winds whisper the name Alexandria," Arenius explained.

"The dream of a kid, that's all it was," Cornelius sputtered, waving him off.

"Would you just stop and listen for once. In the vision, it was as though I was given wings of a bird and guided over vast valleys, lands, and seas. Until I came upon the most beautiful tower I have ever seen. Made of limestone and granite it reached for the sky. An eternal flame burning at its top, bright enough to be seen from the farthest horizon. On shore, I soared past amazing marketplaces, temples, palaces, and roads lined with weird gods having animal heads, to have my vision end at a library. It was filled with innumerable scrolls lining shelves from ceiling to floor," Arenius ended.

Cornelius stopped in his tracks, his face deadpan, "Sounds like the Lighthouse and Library of Alexandria," Cornelius whispered, facing away. Now puzzled, "How could you know of them?"

"That's it, I've been there. And like fighting, somehow, I just know things about it. I feel as though I'm being led to go. Like I'm being pulled by strong waters, only to discover the rivers which I ride upon are mine to choose from."

Cornelius remained silent as he attempted to comprehend how his son was able to describe a city which he had never seen in such detail.

"This is what I'm meant to do. You always wanted me to be something great. Here's my chance," Arenius pleaded.

"But not this. All this is madness," Cornelius assured as he faced his son. "All I wanted was for you to come into your own for the Republic's sake."

"There you go, the Republic! Can't you see the republic is dying, and Augustus is making sure of that. You're so caught up with doing Rome's bidding, you can't see this is who I am. Who I'm chosen to be."

A brief hush enveloped them, their gazes locked in a silent exchange, amidst the bustling symphony of dockside activity that surrounded them.

"It's getting late, we need to find your mother," Cornelius ended, leaving Arenius to himself.

"You will never change," Arenius mutters to himself, following after his father.

XII

Augustus, clad in a regal purple toga, commanded the attention of nine-hundred Senators within the grand Curia Cornelia Senate House in Rome. This four-story structure, a beacon of the Republic's power, loomed impressively over its surroundings on a massive foundation spanning five thousand square feet. Adorned with vast marble slabs, the Curia Cornelia exuded an aura of majesty and authority that resonated throughout the known world.

Stone and wood mosaic fragments adorned the interior walls, narrating Rome's storied past from the triumphant days of subduing the Etruscans to the recent clash at Actium. The floor gleamed with meticulously polished marble, sourced from the finest quarries across the Republic. Towering vaulted ceilings not only lent grandeur but also enhanced the room's acoustics to a standard that could rival even the most renowned amphitheaters. This singular chamber served as a prestigious arena where Rome's upper echelon engaged in impassioned debates, each argument echoing through history in defense of the Republic.

Today, silence enveloped the vast chamber as nine hundred Senators reclined in their ornate seats arranged on the three grand tiers that ran along a side of the edifice. Augustus stood before them, his presence commanding, framed by the majestic Altar of Victory adorned with a gleaming statue of Nike. The goddess, crafted in shimmering gold, stood tall upon a world globe, her outstretched hand offering a laurel wreath symbolizing triumph and glory.

"Senators of the great Republic of Rome, I implore you to take heed of my words. You have honored me with some of the highest titles in our nation's history, in which I'm truly grateful," he briefly paused to stare several of them in their eyes, allowing his words to seep in their ears. "Yet what I do is not for myself but for all of the Senate, which remains the backbone from which Rome is able to stand. And for the citizens of the Republic, who entrust their lives to your wisdom. Therefore, it's from my love of this great city, established by our first King, Romulus, that I must warn you. What we have accomplished since our foundation cannot be undo, however, things cannot go back to how it used to be. Civil wars have been a constant plague to our people as powerful men have fought to take more power, but not I. And as my father Julius Caesar believed, we must not only establish peaceful borders to our growing nation. We must also secure the heart of the Republic and keep it from the hands of tyrants. And as Imperator, and with the aid of my Praetorians, I will not rest until Rome has subdued its enemies within and without. We will have our day of Peace, and it begins now. Hail to the empire," he ended, saluting the Senate with a fist pound to the chest.

The Senate rose in unison, their thunderous applause echoing through the chamber. Voices joined together in a rhythmic chant, "Princeps... Princeps... Princeps," bestowing upon Augustus the esteemed title of First Citizen.

Descending from the elevated platform, the emperor was

flanked by six Praetorian Guards who moved gracefully to his side, their polished armor gleaming under the sunlight. Leading the way were the two foremost soldiers, bearing aloft the majestic eagle standard, its golden wings outstretched and symbolizing not just authority but also a divine endorsement of his rule. Augustus had learned from his predecessors mistake, realizing that by not having personal guards was his undoing. Therefore, he took measures to ensure he would not make the same mistake.

Halfway across the floor, every Senator had united in the chant. A faint smile crept onto Augustus' lips, a silent acknowledgment of his unique achievement as Rome's inaugural Emperor. Satisfied, he strode out through the grand bronze doors of the Senate House into the open air.

Emerging from the shadowed embrace of the towering Ionic columns, Augustus stepped into the blinding embrace of the sun's golden rays. The bustling Forum was a sea of faces, each one alight with fervor and adoration for their newly crowned emperor. The air vibrated with the thunderous chant of "Princeps", echoing off the marble structures that surrounded them. It was a scene of jubilation fit for a conquering hero, yet there were no enemy banners in sight, only colorful ribbons fluttering in the gentle breeze. The crowd swayed to the rhythm of joyful melodies, their jubilant spirits lifting victory paddles high into the air as symbols of their unwavering loyalty and exultation.

Augustus came to a sudden stop, his hand lifting in a graceful arc to acknowledge the vast crowd stretching out before him like a shimmering sea. *"Ah, the fresh winds of change. I am the First Citizen,"* he thought to himself. Walking with a confident stride, he descended the ancient Curia Cornelia steps, his hands elegantly clasped behind his back, exuding the aura of someone who had just achieved great success.

Additional Praetorian Guards with their pristine armor, stood in precise formation along both sides of the marble steps. Each guard's gladius hung menacingly from their belts, while their scutum shields were gripped firmly in their free hands. As Augustus made his way down the staircase, the guards flanked him closely, creating a protective barrier around him. Suddenly, a soldier emerged from the crowd and advanced towards him.

"Emperor Augustus," he saluted, bowing his head.

"All shall salute me and bow at the feet of Izraga," he thought, taking another moment to enjoy his new title. "What is it, soldier?" he questioned to the still bowing soldier.

"I have a word on General Cornelius," the soldier reported, bringing himself perfectly upright.

"Fall in and debrief," Augustus said, as he walked down the stairs with purpose, Augustus noticed his original six guards being joined by the sentinels who had been stationed at the entrance of the Curia Julia.

A line of guards, reflected the sunlight like liquid gold, led the way through the bustling throng. Their synchronized steps parted the crowd effortlessly, not a single person dared to stray into their path. Each guard bore a symbol of Rome's power on their chest, handpicked by Augustus himself for their unwavering loyalty. It wasn't just skill that set them apart; it was the fierce determination etched into their faces, a silent promise to lay down their lives for their emperor. The air crackled with tension, warning any foolhardy soul against challenging the impenetrable wall of protection around their ruler.

"Yes sir," the guard shouted over the crowd and swiftly fell in line beside his emperor.

Augustus stood tall, his presence commanding as the bustling crowd instinctively made way for him, a silent testament to his undeniable authority and sway over the people.

"For your sake, this better be important enough to disturb my celebrations," Augustus continued.

"I believe it is sir," the soldier responded confidently.

"Well deliver the message," he demanded, saluting the people as they walked.

"Cornelius-," was all the soldier could say before Augustus shot the soldier a death stare. "I meant, General Cornelius, was spotted in Ostia's markets before boarding an outbound ship."

"Did the sentinel engage the target in the markets?"

"No sir, they stated they were alone at the time."

"In that case, I want them silenced."

"Immediately, I will be sure to have some men interrogate the Dock Master for answers. And learn where the vessel is heading."

"No, I was referring to the sentinel," Augustus replied, keeping his gaze ahead of him. "I will not accept weakness. And being alone is an excuse of the weak, and will not be tolerated in my presence." The guard became silent, shuttering at his leader's words. "Is there anything else to report?" Augustus's gaze remained fixed ahead, his focus unwavering.

"No sir."

"Then you're dismissed," Augustus ordered, stopping in his tracks to allow the soldier to salute and step away. "One last thing, make sure the Light Bringer's, light, is quenched permanently," he added, getting the soldier to pause. "Remember, failure is not an option."

"Yes, Princeps," the soldier replied then saluted, before walking away to complete his orders.

Augustus watched the soldier disappear into the bustling

crowd. After taking a moment to enjoy the festive atmosphere, he continued his march with his security team at his side.

129

XIII

Floriana's gaze lingered on her son's captivating hazel eyes, gently brushing aside the tousled strands of hair that swayed in the breeze across his face. "Simply because someone fails to perceive your true essence does not diminish who you are," she affirmed with a maternal smile.

Arenius furrowed his brow in confusion, seeking clarity as she continued, "Marriage to your father did not guarantee his respect; it had to be earned. Being wedded to one of Rome's esteemed generals is no small feat, especially for a non-Roman like me." She disclosed her origins, "My family hails from an ancient and noble city in Greece - Sparta."

"Are you Spartan?" Arenius asked eagerly.

"Yes, you carry noble blood not just from your father. Although my city now exists as a mere echo of its past glory, it does not diminish my warrior spirit. That is why I learned the ways of the shield and blade as tradition dictates," With pride shining in her eyes, she revealed the gleaming hilt of her sword by lifting the edge of her cloak. With a fluid motion, she drew out the sword from its leather sheath and presented it. The setting sun bathed the steel blade in a warm orange hue, casting a mesmerizing sight.

"So that's how you possessed fighting skills. I never witnessed your training sessions," Arenius exclaimed with youthful enthusiasm.

At sea for a week now, Arenius stood by the stern railing of the Adresta, captivated by a majestic falcon swooping down into the shimmering depths in search of its next meal. The Adresta, fashioned in the classic style of a corbita, was a swift single-mast merchant ship slicing through the waves with grace.

Numerous moons had journeyed across the sky since their departure from Ostia, and the confined space below deck had grown stifling with its stagnant atmosphere. The deck above beckoned with its invigorating freshness. Arenius immersed himself in the intricate dance of operating a ship, marveling at the taut rigging and billowing sails, and admiring the diligent crew that tirelessly tended to them. Eagerly anticipating his daily reprieve, he awaited the captain's designated time for them to emerge above deck, a precious window when the ocean lay calm. These stolen moments offered him a chance to inhale the rejuvenating salty breeze and absorb the mesmerizing expanse of the sea.

"Beautiful, aren't they?" stepping closer to him, Floriana stood by his side, her gaze fixed on the falcon as it plummeted towards its target, elegantly spreading its wings at the last second to grasp the prey with its sharp talons. "It's amazing how such a small creature can be an unmatched hunter," facing him. "It's only been a couple of days, and you can barely see your bruise. Something like that would take me weeks to get rid of," eyeing his face.

"Why do I sense there's something you're trying to tell me?" Arenius asked, finally turning his gaze to her.

Floriana's gaze lingered on her son's mesmerizing hazel eyes, delicately sweeping aside the tousled strands of hair that danced in the wind across his face, "Just because someone doesn't see or recognize who you really are, doesn't make who you truly are any less," she confirmed, giving her motherly smile.

"That's easy for you to say, you married him."

"Being married to your father does not mean I automatically had his respect, that part was earned. Being married to one of Rome's greatest generals is not an easy task. Especially when you're not Roman born," Arenius's brows furrowed in confusion, his eyes searching for clarity as she elaborated on the details. "I never told you my family are not Roman by birth, we are from an ancient and noble city in Greece, the city of Sparta."

"You're Spartan?" he questioned excitedly.

"Yes, you come from noble blood, not only from your father. Though my city is only a shadow of its former self, it doesn't make me any less of a warrior. Therefore, I needed to know how to wield a shield and blade as tradition calls for," With pride, she lifted the edge of her cloak, unveiling the gleaming hilt of her sword.

With a graceful motion, she delicately drew the sword from its leather casing and extended it . The setting sun painted the steel blade with a warm orange glow, creating a mesmerizing spectacle.

"That's how you knew how to fight. I couldn't think of a time I saw you training," his excitement, giving evidence of his youth. His eyes sparkled like freshly polished emeralds, widening with a youthful exuberance that spilled over in his animated gestures.

"Yes, during the day like all things, I had to teach myself how to serve your father. Yet the night belongs to me and for years I kept up my training. What do you really think made me attractive to your father other than my charming personality? she smiled charmingly. "But even with that, even he would not admit I bested him in a duel in our younger years."

"That sounds like him, alright," he mocked, getting them to laugh. "Now you have to tell me everything," Arenius smiled.

"Well, before me and your father were courted and before he was the great man he is now. The legion he was then a part of was stationed on the outskirts of Sparta. When one day, he and a couple of his countrymen walked into my training pit. Of course, they mocked the girls and I for training as women. Saying it's not a woman's job to fight, and how it should be left to the men."

"What did you say to him?" Arenius said, giving her his full attention.

"It's not what I said, but what I did that matters. We wagered, if I were to lose in a friendly sparring match, I would close the pit, that had been open for generations. Granted I was the one keeping the pit open. He also want me to have a meal with him."

"What happened if lost?"

"If he lost, he and his men would leave the pit and never return."

"What happened next?"

"The only thing which could happen. Till this day, I'm not sure which choice would have been worse; allowing your father to win or the pit having to close? After he was no longer allowed in the pit, he stalked me around the city for days asking for my name. It was actually charming and dare I say, amusing, to see how much he would endure to get it," she laughed.

"I would have loved to seen that," Arenius continued, grinning from ear to ear.

"Well, you have already. Your father has changed little since then and that is what I love about him. He always remains focused and goes all in for what he believes in," resting her hands gently on his, she leaned in closer while he balanced on the railing.

"That's the problem, he has never put much effort in anything concerning me. In his eyes I'm nothing but a burden to the family," he contested, pulling away his hand.

"Don't say that. I know your father has his ways, but that does not mean he doesn't see who you really are. And if he doesn't, then give him time to see the handsome and strong person you are becoming," she said, pulling him in for a hug.

Attempting to break free, he found himself ensnared in her unyielding grasp. As she sensed his internal conflict melting away, he reciprocated by enveloping her in a tight embrace. Together, they turned towards the west, witnessing Phoebus guiding his sun chariot as it finished it descend beneath the rippling horizon.

XIV

The voyage spanning nearly three weeks from Ostia to Alexandria unfolded like a carefully choreographed dance on the sea. The wind, at times gentle and other times fierce, pushed against the ship, guiding it from port to port. Amidst the rhythmic creaking of the wooden vessel, the captain stood tall in the center of the deck, his weathered face illuminated by the sun as he bellowed out precise commands that mingled with the salty air.

Responding to his orders with practiced expertise, the crew moved swiftly and purposefully across the deck. The Vesta family, drawn by curiosity and a desire to witness the intricate workings of the ship, ascended to the upper deck where they were met with a scene of organized chaos. The crew members, their muscles taut and glistening with sweat under the sun's relentless gaze, maneuvered ropes and sails with a fluidity that mesmerized onlookers.

Arenius watched in awe as each sailor navigated their tasks with a grace that belied the harshness of their environment. They swung from mast to rigging like agile acrobats, adjusting rigging and securing lines with a precision that spoke of years spent at sea. It was a symphony of movement and skill, where every gesture and action seemed perfectly timed and executed, painting a portrait of seafaring mastery that left Arenius breathless with admiration.

Arenius rested his elbows on the guard rail, once again taking in the sun dipping low in the sky. There was something about being on the open sea which demanded peace; the cool wind, the creeks of the sails and mast, or simply how the ship gracefully glided across the seas as the blue Mediterranean waves bashed against the haul. Whatever it was, he was thankful to have experienced it all, as it helped to bring peace and clarify his purpose.

"There she is, the Pharos," Cornelius informed, standing at Arenius' side, Floriana at the other. "The once proud symbol of Egypt. May her light shed light on your journey," he continued, staring out at the distant city in awe.

Glistening like a flawless pearl in the sunlight, the obelisk-shaped lighthouse rose majestically from the glistening waters like a reborn phoenix. Positioned on a narrow spit of land extending into the Mediterranean Sea from Alexandria's bustling harbor, the Pharos Lighthouse was a tribute to architectural marvels post-Alexander the Great. Reaching an impressive height of one hundred and eighty-seven feet, its square foundation spanned almost twice the length of two mighty Roman warships. Crafted meticulously to cast its radiant beacon across vast distances on tranquil seas, this structure demanded admiration at noon when sunlight danced off its polished limestone and granite facade. The very construction of this masterpiece stood as a lasting testament to Egypt's unparalleled craftsmanship.

Employing an intricate system of pulleys, the crew on Adresta's ship expertly guided it towards the dock, securing it seamlessly in place. As they finished the docking process, Cornelius exchanged a few hushed words with Adresta's captain before leading his family off the vessel. They draped their cloaks over their heads, concealing their features to evade detection by any harbor workers, particularly the vigilant Roman soldiers who were strategically positioned around the area.

In order to arrive at the Library of Alexandria, they had to trek through broad paved roads, weave through the vibrant marketplace, and navigate the remnants of the ancient royal residences without drawing attention. If Cornelius hadn't been renowned as the fearless leader in the historic Battle of Actium, blending in wouldn't have posed such a challenge amidst the diverse crowd speaking different tongues. For the Battle of Actium did mark the decisive downfall of Egypt's dynastic rule, solidifying Cornelius' place in history.

Alexandria bustled with the organized chaos of a meticulously designed city. Its streets reverberated with a cacophony of voices as merchants, sheltered under elegant stone arcades and impromptu canvas shelters, enthusiastically hawked their wares to the transient crowds strolling past.

Amongst the towering spires and intricate carvings that adorned the city, Arenius beheld a mesmerizing tapestry of cultures converging at the bustling harbor. In contrast to the Roman politicians' portrayal of Egypt as a savage and desolate realm, Arenius found himself immersed in a vibrant land teeming with life and diversity. The sight of individuals hailing from distant kingdoms mingling harmoniously in this cosmopolitan hub left an indelible impression on him, reshaping his perceptions with each passing moment.

Arenius stood mesmerized by the peculiar individuals adorned with metallic studs in intricate patterns on their noses, ears, and even lips. The symphony of diverse languages swirling around him was a melodic tapestry weaving through his senses. The kaleidoscope of skin hues captivated him, from alabaster pale to ebony dark, each shade a vibrant testament to the world's rich diversity.

He could not help but wonder, if Rome was willing to deceive its citizens on trivial matters, what other falsehoods had they spread? As he explored the world firsthand, he grew determined to scrutinize everything he had learned, pondering whether Rome truly stood as a guiding star in a shadowed realm.

The unfamiliar warmth of the land began to embrace him, its beauty gradually captivating his senses. Contrary to his initial expectations of desolation, he found himself surrounded by exquisite fountains, shimmering pools mirroring the sky, and vibrant palm and tamarisk trees embellishing every corner of the bustling city and the opulent Royal Quarter. This luxurious display hinted at the grandeur that defined Egypt, offering a glimpse into why this ancient realm had stood strong for countless centuries.

Following a short respite to revive their spirits with plump dates, succulent grilled fish, and crisp water procured from the marketplace, they sought refuge beneath the sprawling canopy of a majestic tree. As twilight descended, cloaked in shadows, the Vesta family stealthily approached their destination - the illustrious Library of Alexandria, known as the Capital of Knowledge - evading detection with practiced ease.

The library sprawled across an expanse that dwarfed the Roman forum, its central dome soaring to a height equivalent to eight stories. The magnificent structure was divided into four distinct parts: the imposing hypostyle hall at the entrance, the majestic rotunda positioned in the heart of the complex, the secluded rear chamber, and two sheltered colonnade walkways that stretched out like elegant wings on each side of the rotunda. These colonnades elegantly intertwined at the end of the chamber, giving rise to expansive courtyards on either side of the library. When observed from above, the entire library complex took on the shape of a cross embellished with a radiant halo at its core - embodied by the resplendent rotunda.

"This completely outdoes anything in Rome and puts the Temple of Mercury to shame," Arenius thought as they approached the hypostyle hall.

The hypostyle hall was meant to awe on lookers and draw crowds to its grand entrance. Massive columns resembling towering trees supported its roof, their surfaces adorned with vibrant hues of purple, blue, and green. Each column loomed as wide as a grown person is tall. Passing through the colossal pillars marked a transition into a hallowed space, silently urging visitors to adopt a demeanor befitting the sacredness of the surroundings.

Arenius moved with a hushed reverence through the maze of towering columns that heralded the entrance to the library's labyrinthine depths. It felt as though he had wandered into an ancient sacred grove, where the majestic stone pillars rose like petrified trees, their tops vanishing into the shadowy heights above.

Quietly, with measured steps, they neared the library's entrance, concealed from the prying eyes of the heavens above. The only sound that broke the silence was the melodious symphony of birdsong reverberating in the dark alcoves of the lofty ceiling. As they stood before the imposing twin doors of the library, Cornelius reached out for one of the intricately crafted bronze handles fashioned in the likeness of menacing King Cobras, their scales glistening in the muted light. With a firm grip, he tugged on the majestic serpent's hood, anticipating resistance. However, to his surprise, not even a fraction of movement stirred within the stubborn door.

"Must be locked from the inside," Cornelius muttered, giving the door another tug.

"Let me try," Arenius said, proudly stepping forward.

"Let's not do that. Knowing you, the entire door may be ripped from its frame," Cornelius warned against any further examination of the door.

"And that would be bad, how?" Arenius asked.

"Since the door is locked from within, someone must be inside. If we plan on entering, we probably don't want to let the world know we're doing it," Cornelius replied.

Arenius thought on his father's words, before nodding in agreement.

"What's next then?" Floriana asked.

Cornelius took a slow, deliberate breath as he pondered, "For now, we walk the rest of the complex and see what we find."

Retracing their steps through the grand hypostyle hall, they carefully explored the outer facade of the ancient complex. Arenius' keen eyes caught sight of the soft of a flame escaping through a row of precisely carved square windows, serving as both ventilation and natural light sources. These unique windows adorned the upper section of the rotunda, nestled just below the intricate eaves of the roof.

"I can get in from there," Arenius gestured towards the window, drawing the attention of the others.

"You'll need wings to reach them," Floriana said.

"If we all cannot get in, no one goes. Besides, those ports are at least thirty-five feet from the ground. Do you even know if you'll make that jump?" Cornelius questioned.

"I don't, but there's only one way to find out," Arenius continued, Cornelius staring on, not convinced. "Don't worry. I plan on reaching the windows by climbing the colonnade. That will get me at least halfway up, and I believe I can make the jump to the port from there. Once inside I'll find a way to unlock the door and let you in through the front."

"That's ridiculous, no way we are letting you go alone," Cornelius's voice barely above a breath.

"Cornelius, if we are to get in before sunrise, you have to allow him to try. We have no other options," Floriana insisted, resting a hand on his forearm. "You have to let him go. I know he can do it, and I believe you think the same."

Arenius stood still, anticipation hanging heavy in the air for his their reply.

"Fine," Cornelius relented. "But if anything goes wrong or you sense something out of the ordinary. You get out of there right away, no lingering back. Is that understood?"

"Understood," Arenius agreed.

Removing his cloak with a swift gesture, he readied himself to take the initial step towards scaling the rooftop of the elegant colonnade walkway.

"Hold on, Arenius, let your father and I check to make sure it's clear. We wouldn't want others to see you doing what in other words should be impossible. May be disturbing to say the least," Floriana chimed in.

Arenius's lips curved up in a soft smile, acknowledging the depth of his mother's insight as she and Cornelius strolled over to examine the surroundings. Despite the library's central location within the bustling city, as evening descended and the heavy doors shut with a resounding thud, an eerie stillness settled over the grounds, turning it into a deserted wasteland. Yet, they knew all too well that it was crucial for them to maintain this desolate facade.

Staying concealed within the veil of darkness, Arenius cautiously positioned himself a few strides away from the colonnade, ensuring an unobstructed path lay before him. He awaited a subtle cue from each of his parents, and as they materialized gracefully from their hidden alcoves behind the stately columns, signaling him forward, he drew in a series of steadying breaths. Fixing his gaze steadily upon the elevated roof of the walkway, perched ten feet above ground level, he propelled himself into motion with agile swiftness.

Within moments, he closed the gap swiftly, narrowly avoiding a collision with a looming column. With a powerful leap at the last instant, he launched himself airborne. Drifting through the ethereal expanse with the gentle touch of the sea breeze tenderly brushing against his youthful countenance, he experienced a weightless sensation akin to that of a drifting feather as time seemed to stretch infinitely. And in an instant that lingered like eternity, he made contact with the terracotta roof with a resounding CRUNCH, shattering several crimson-hued tiles beneath his impact.

Bathed in the silvery glow of the moon, Arenius stood tall, his muscles taut with accomplishment as he effortlessly soared over atop the towering walkway that stood ten feet high. In that moment, he couldn't deny the exhilarating rush of power that surged through him as a Light Bringer.

"Why are you standing there like sheep at a water hole? Yes, you can jump high, now get going," Cornelius yelled with a whisper from below.

Arenius, his gaze steady and determined, recalibrated his focus. Surveying the vast expanse between him and the window, he noted its elevated position compared to his last daring leap. Mimicking his previous actions with precision, Arenius took a step back and propelled himself forward in a powerful sprint. The tiles beneath his feet groaned under the pressure of his speed. Assessing the distance meticulously, his eyes darted between the intricate details of the rotunda's outer wall and the lofty window looming above. As he closed in on his target, mere feet away from the wall, he launched himself into the air with unwavering resolve.

Moving with a silent grace towards the looming wall, he executed a precise maneuver, planting his foot firmly against the rough surface. The forceful push propelled him upwards, granting him the necessary momentum to reach for the window. Suspended at the peak of his leap, his outstretched hand grasped onto the weathered ledge. With a vice-like grip and a heart-stopping thirty-five feet drop below, he clung on tenaciously, stealing a fleeting glance downwards at his fretting parents.

Hanging perilously from the windowsill for agonizing moments, he hoisted himself up and vanished into the darkness beyond. Cornelius and Floriana exhaled in unison, their tense expressions melting into relieved smiles.

XV

Concealed amidst the looming darkness cast by the library's towering marble columns, Cornelius and Floriana crouched by the grand entrance. Time seemed to stretch endlessly as they anxiously lingered there, their hearts pounding in anticipation. Arenius had disappeared through the ornate upper windows into the library, leaving them in a tense silence broken only by the faint rustle of their own movements. Desperate for any sign of his progress, they leaned closer to the colossal wooden doors, straining to catch even the slightest whisper from beyond.

"I told you it was a bad idea to send him in only. He wasn't ready, and if something happened to him there's no way for us to get to him," Cornelius whispered in the shadows.

Floriana wanted to calm him, but she herself was beginning to doubt if sending their son in alone was the best decision. "We have to allow him to try."

"At the cost of his life, Floriana? Fighting for your homeland is one thing, fighting in some bizarre spirit war is another. He hasn't even had the chance to experience life."

"Have you given it any thought, that maybe this is how he comes to experience it. But we will never know unless we give him a chance. Instead of keeping him close, maybe try letting him go for a change."

Cornelius sighed heavily, resting his head and back against the column, "You remember all those times you begged me not to return to the front and to remain with you and Arenius. Truth is, it's much easier being a soldier than being a husband or father. All I know is war. And no soldier wants to bring war home to his home, regardless how hard it is to keep it from not happening. Tell me how can I keep war away when I've been the Republic's offspring of death and pain for years now? When I close my eyes, it's not your faces I see, but the faces of all I've slain, beckoning me back to the ongoing battlefield," Cornelius ended, his face bleak and partially hidden by shadow.

"Cornelius, my love," moving nearer to him, she inched into the darkness, her presence barely discernible. "You must understand that Arenius and I, know things aren't easy for you. But somehow you manage to stay strong for us. We accept you as you are, especially Arenius, flaws and all. Why? Because he sees you and all you have accomplished. He only wants to see more of you, not as the next great general of the Republic, but as his father. It's not what you say to him, but what you do with him which makes an impression," she pauses, hearing nearby voices that eventually dissipate in the distance. "Our son may be some sort of demi-god. I can't believe I can say that," she continued, laughing at the thought. "What matters is that, deep inside and without a doubt, he'll trade it all for you."

Cornelius fell into a contemplative silence, his mind swirling with thoughts of the uncertain future if anything were to befall Arenius. Perhaps the solution lay in releasing him to forge his own path. As he pondered this, a faint shuffling noise emanated from within, prompting Cornelius to swiftly retreat into the concealment of the shadows. A heavy dragging sound reverberated through the air on the other side of the door, causing Cornelius to grasp his sword firmly, poised for action with it raised at shoulder level. Gradually, the door began to creak open on its massive hinges, filling the space with eerie echoes that bounced off the imposing Doric columns. Despite the dimness of the surroundings, there was just enough moonlight filtering in for Cornelius to discern Floriana's tense form beside him, her weapon gleaming as she readied herself for any potential threat ahead.

"Ma, Pa, you there," Arenius whispered, peeking out between the doors.

"Arenius," Floriana exhaled, sheathing her weapon to run and hug him.

"What took you so long?" Cornelius questioned.

"You'll see once inside, come quick," he answered, waving them in.

Cornelius carefully surveyed the surroundings for any signs of a tail before leading the group into the library. Inside, Arenius swiftly moved to shut the door, catching Cornelius's attention as he effortlessly hoisted a hefty wooden security beam and secured it across the entrance. The beam stretched across the wide double doors, its solid structure hinting at its weight of nearly two hundred pounds.

Having the beam secured in place, Arenius brushed off his hands, "I guess this is my life now," he said, turning, to see Cornelius staring at him with a surprising awe.

"I would have to agree," Cornelius agreed.

"I see why it took you so long to open the door, this place is beautiful," Floriana chimed in, gazing out at the library before them.

Venturing deeper into the library, they were greeted by a display of opulence and grandeur that spoke volumes about the former glory of the Ptolemaic Empire. The circular room was lined with towering shelves in three tiers, ascending towards the lofty sixty-foot ceiling like colossal steps adorned with ancient scrolls. At intervals of twenty feet, sturdy wooden ladders leaned against the shelves, offering access to a treasure trove of papyri scrolls, tablets, and parchments arranged on higher levels. Elaborate frescoes depicting the Ibis-headed Thoth, the Egyptian deity revered for wisdom and writing, embellished every available inch of wall space. This lavish decoration left no doubt as to why this repository had earned its prestigious moniker as the Epicenter of Wisdom.

The moment one stepped into the library, they were greeted by intricate painted frescoes adorning the walls and an extensive collection of scrolls. However, what truly captured everyone's attention was the centerpiece hanging from the domed ceiling. Like a radiant sun suspended in mid-air, a colossal twenty-foot-wide sphere coated in pure gold dangled from above. Crafted with a sturdy wooden frame encasing its core and embellished with the most exquisite gold known to the ancient realm, it was a spectacle beyond compare.

Every inch of its golden surface was adorned with meticulous etchings, elaborate carvings, and vibrant paintings that narrated the epic tale of kings. The scenes depicted Thoth, the guardian deity, shielding the mighty Queen Isis following the treacherous murder of her husband Osiris by his own brother Seth. Illustrated on this magnificent sphere was also the moment when Thoth tended to Horus, the avenging Falcon god who sought justice for his father's tragic demise.

Beneath the shimmering orb rested a grand brazier, its flickering flames dancing in mesmerizing patterns that bathed the celestial sphere in a warm, ethereal glow, enveloping every crevice of the ancient, cavernous chamber in a radiant golden light.

"It makes you wonder, how kingdoms can be constantly at war, yet have time to create wonders such as this," Floriana marveled as she took in the library's grandeur.

"Sorry to say, it's because of wonders such as this, that men fight. Only the wealthy kingdoms of the world can construct such structures. Wherever there is wealth, an army is needed to protect that wealth. And if there is a need to protect it, that means another wants what you have," Cornelius casually remarked, his eyes fixed on the radiant orb gliding gracefully in the sky.

"You would think great knowledge would lead the world to seek out peaceful means of solving their differences or better - listen to what another has to say," Arenius added, studying Cornelius whose eyes stayed ahead.

"Well, a great philosopher once said, '*The only true wisdom consists in knowing that you know nothing.*' Kingdoms fight because knowledge is not what they seek, men seek power and glory, not-," before he could complete his sentence, his gaze was drawn to the Roman soldier sprawled unconscious on the ground, partially obscured by the flickering flames of the brazier.

Floriana and Cornelius promptly turned to Arenius, who simply shrugged "You were right, there were guards inside," he said before continuing further into the library.

Briefly, Cornelius and Floriana exchanged a knowing look at the unconscious man, then shared a shrug before following Arenius from behind.

Flawlessly, Arenius led them pass the flickering flames of the brazier, to the far end of the circular chamber, directly across from where they had entered. With purposeful strides, he halted before a scroll shelf. To the uninitiated observer, this specific shelf blended seamlessly with its counterparts, offering no immediate clues to its significance.

"Where do we go from here? Hope we didn't travel all this way for a scroll." Cornelius questioned.

Ignoring their words, Arenius cocked his head slightly and fixed his eyes on a mysterious object nestled at the far end of the cluttered shelf. With deliberate movements, he reached out, displacing a pile of ancient scrolls before delicately running his fingers along the rough surface of the shelf's back wall. As his fingertips brushed against a distinct groove etched into the wood, a sense of recognition tingled through him. Retracting his hand slowly, he drew his gladius from its scabbard with a fluid motion.

"What is it?" Floriana questioned.

"I think it's a key," Arenius muttered.

"What's a key?" Cornelius followed up, still puzzled at what was happening.

Clutching the shimmering amethyst gem tightly with his fingertips, it unclasped effortlessly from its position on the sword's hilt, almost as if it sensed its intended removal. Arenius delicately placed the radiant stone into the intricately carved crevice and took a step back, uncertainty clouding his features. The vivid vision that had led him to this moment merely pointed to the shelf, leaving him in anticipation. He half-expected a mystical voice to offer guidance, mirroring ancient legends. Yet, the air remained still, enveloped in an eerie silence that echoed through the chamber.

"I guess your Divine Speaker is not so divine after all," Cornelius stated.

A sudden thunderous noise reverberated through the library. The air filled with a deliberate, rhythmic clinking sound, reminiscent of mechanical gears turning. The clatter grew louder, accompanied by the grating noise of rough stone scraping against the floor until the lowest row of shelves shifted abruptly with a resounding thud. Shortly after, the shelving unit started to pivot back on massive steel hinges, opening a passage that unleashed a chilly and stale gust from within the hidden depths.

Floriana smirked at Cornelius, "At this point, I'd stop questioning things if I were you."

"Alright. I get it, don't have to rub salt in the wound," Cornelius responded before striding towards the massive brazier. He retrieved a flaming stick from it and proceeded to light the unlit torch resting by the entrance, casting a warm glow in the dim space. "Here you go Light Bringer, I think this is what you came to," handing the torch over to Arenius. "Even generals can be wrong now and then."

"Thanks, Pa," Arenius said respectfully.

With the oiled torch held aloft, Arenius confronts the shadows, casting light upon a serpentine stone stairway descending into the unknown depths. Prior to proceeding further, he carefully plucks the amethyst gem from its resting place in the shelf, inhaling deeply before embarking on his gradual journey downward. The weighty shelf behind him creaks shut, enclosing them in an ominous embrace.

XVI

Every footfall carried them deeper into a corridor cloaked in musty, cool air that caressed their flesh with a chilling touch. The flickering torchlight cast playful shadows on the winding passageway until they stumbled upon enigmatic symbols meticulously carved into a stone niche.

"I wonder what all this means," Floriana asked aloud, her fingers tracing the strange characters.

Stopping in his tracks, Arenius faced his parents, "What do you mean? It reads, '*Foul of the night, return to the Nether,*' on both sides of the wall. Must be here to keep demons out. It's the same saying etched into my sword. Do you not see the light emanating from them either?"

"There's no light. Besides, we are able to read what's on your sword, that's our language. But this," Floriana gestures to the wall, "I have never seen."

"*Phhf*, to us, it's no different than the tongues of the barbarians," Cornelius added.

"This is amazing," Arenius said ecstatically, turning to continue his descent, more excitement in each step.

"You're telling us, you can read this non-sense?" he asked, waving his fingers at the puzzling glyphs.

"Every word," Arenius beamed.

Spiraling down through the narrow stone staircase, their journey felt endless until they arrived at a hidden chamber deep beneath the library. Emerging onto a spacious landing, the flickering torch in their hands struggled to push back the thick darkness that enveloped them, barely illuminating the ancient walls adorned with intricate carvings.

"Where are we?" Floriana asked no one in particular.

"I guess somewhere beneath the library," Cornelius responded dryly.

"I figured that much," her eyes attempting to pierce through the veil of darkness. "And I meant, where are we?" She quipped.

"Not sure, we must allow the light to show us," Arenius mumbled, spotting a brazier to the left of the stairs.

Maneuvering around his parents with nimble steps, he drew closer to the brazier. Instead of the expected crackling wood or glowing coal, it held a mysterious mixture of grainy gray and black matter. Intrigued, he reached out and scooped up a handful of the enigmatic substance, feeling its texture like fine sand slipping through his fingers. Curiously, he brought it to his nose but was met with an absence of any discernible scent. Puzzled by this unfamiliar find, he watched as the grains cascaded through his open palm, cascading back into the depths of the brazier like a gentle waterfall returning to its source.

"*If it's in the brazier, it can be lit. Only one way to find out,*" Leaning back from the crackling brazier, he extended his torch to make contact with the mysterious substance.

In an instant, the flames eagerly embraced the mysterious concoction, casting a luminous glow across their shadowed realm. A stone conduit linked to the brassiere brimmed with those identical rare elements, their gazes tracing the fiery path as it meandered to the left along the aged wall. Reaching a corner at a distance of thirty feet, it gracefully descended at a forty-five-degree angle towards a lower tier, its radiant illumination unveiling an array of ancient artifacts from epochs long preceding the dawn of the Roman Republic.

Descending through the chamber, the flames danced hungrily, enveloping the expansive rectangular space until they completed their circuit on the right side near the staircase's base, setting ablaze the last brazier. In a mere heartbeat, the ancient room burst into a mesmerizing display of shimmering golden embers. Revealed before them now was a grand platform, flanked by twin stone steps cascading down to a lower level where an array of artifacts from distant lands and mysterious origins were meticulously arranged. The treasures adorned the walls and alcoves, whispering tales of forgotten civilizations and untold adventures.

Exotic weaponry and gleaming armor adorned the walls and hung from ornate racks like prized possessions, each piece telling a story of battles won. Scrolls, their edges delicately rolled, were meticulously arranged on sturdy oak shelves. Dominating the room was a square arena filled with fine sand, where wooden mannequins stood tall atop posts buried deeply within the granules. Time-worn scars marred their once-smooth surfaces, evidence of countless hours of training and dedication etched into their very being.

In front of them, commanding the attention of all who entered, loomed a sleek podium stretching elegantly across the platform. Crafted meticulously from a solitary block of pristine alabaster, the podium boasted intricate carvings that depicted six valiant warriors locked in combat with a fearsome seven-headed Hydra. Each serpentine head sported a regal diadem fashioned to resemble radiant sunbeams. The final tableau captured one warrior victoriously perched atop the colossal monster's lifeless form, having just severed its final menacing head.

"I can't believe my eyes," Floriana gasped in awe.

"How could such treasure be kept secret for so long?" Cornelius asked as they all approached the podium.

"Not sure, but I have the feeling this might give us some answers," Arenius carefully unraveled a pair of vibrant crimson silk threads that tightly secured the massive scroll.

The ancient scroll exuded a faint scent of aged parchment, its surface smooth and unblemished as if time itself had preserved it meticulously. With delicate reverence, Arenius unfurled the scroll, revealing a mesmerizing tapestry of warriors locked in combat with grotesque beasts that varied in size from petite birds to colossal warships. The glyphs etched in shimmering golden ink mirrored the intricate carvings on the spiral stairwell, each symbol pulsating with an otherworldly glow as if infused with ancient magic.

"Can you tell us what it says?" Curious, Floriana questioned Arenius, delicately running her finger over the intricate inked symbols.

At the farthest edge of the platform, as the scroll unfurled completely, "I'll do my best. The first words read, 'Here I write the names and history of the Light Bearers. By their strength and blade, they shall bring balance to light and dark'."

Cornelius, stood shoulder to shoulder with Floriana, her delicate fingers caressing the hem of her cloak. The room's flames flickering as Arenius began to recite the ancient text.

"Before there was time, only eternity existed. There was nothing but

light, darkness, and The One, who bent them both to its will. The earth was formed, and mankind was formed to protect and govern it. Yet, when their life cycle ended, they were greeted by the Luminaries, who were created by The One to guide their deceased souls back to the realm of eternity and rejoin with The One.

During this time, there was balance and life. There was peace and abundance throughout all which existed. But as mankind started to fight and wage war, to possess more of what was already given free. Many Luminaries became angry and even envious of mankind. For mankind had gained much through barbarous acts, yet The One stood by and watched.

It was then that Izraga, the highest-ranking Luminary, decided humans were holding his kind back, keeping them from experiencing the splendors of what The One had created, earth. To prove their point, Izraga with many of its chief and fellow Luminaries, abandoned their duties of escorting mankind into eternity. To break into the mortal realm simply to enjoy its spoils, by overthrowing mankind. With their actions, the balance of earth had been upset.

These fallen Luminaries are called by many names in earth's many tongues, yet the phrase demon rings across all. Using their dimensional abilities, these demons began influencing mankind, by inhabiting their bodies, so they too may indulge in the fatness which earth supplied, while simultaneously driving mankind to their destruction.

In order to remain in the human world, Luminaries needed a human willing to say the incantations to welcome the demon into the body. Unfortunately, chief demons possess the strength to enter the human world without the need of a human. However, they cannot remain permanently, the stronger the demon the longer they can linger.

Before creation spun out of control, and darkness began to over-

whelmed the light. The One saw from eternity and acknowledged what the fallen Luminaries were doing to its creation and decided to give mankind the ability to defend themselves. Both mankind and demons were The One's creations. Vowing not to punish those Luminaries which had upset the balance, The One gave those Luminaries time to restore balance back to earth. But they refused, branding themselves as demons. Therefore, The One crafted six stones of Jade, Topaz, Onyx, Obsidian, Amethyst, and lapis lazuli. These stones were to be given to mankind's heroes; to those the stones deemed worthy. Throughout the ages, the stones sought out and awakened many Light Bringers.

It has been prophesied, when all six Light Bringers unify and stand against demons together, then and only then will the power of demons be banished from the realm of earth. And for their heinous acts, the demons are expelled into the Nether never to see light, earth, or The One again, but remain forever in darkness. This marks the restoration, order, and balance to all things."

Surrounded by the crackling flames, the three of them remained fixated on the ancient scroll, delving into its complex details.

"This scroll has every demon and every Light Bringer who encountered them. *Anath, Gilgamesh, Isis, Nimrod, Utanapish-tim, Deborah, Horus, Rabbenu, Achilles, and Moshe,*" Arenius explained.

"Isis, Horus, Achilles, this can't be. I thought they were all legends," Cornelius said in disbelief.

"If we weren't standing in this room, I would be with you, love," Floriana reassured, gently caressing his arm.

"How is this," his finger stopping at the end of the list. "Here, take a look." Cornelius and Floriana simply stared at him. "Right, you can't read it. Well, it says, 'Arenius Vesta.' And it's written in the same hand as the one who wrote the rest of the scroll."

"So, you're saying the same person that wrote the scroll, which was written eons ago, also wrote your name in it?" Floriana questioned.

"I don't know what I'm saying. All I know is that this scroll is old, way older than any of us. Yet my name is written here!"

"I guess that means one thing, like them, you are meant to leave your mark," Cornelius added, placing a hand on Arenius' shoulder. "I know I haven't given you a chance at much, but these last few days have shown me my many errors. But now I'm starting to see you clearly." Arenius smiled.

"I have waited for this moment for so long," Floriana said, giving a group hug.

"Only you could turn a manly moment into this," Cornelius quipped, dropping his head.

"Is that what you call it?"

"Oh, there's something else I came across," Arenius continued, back tracking across the scroll. "The seven-headed hydra, Izraga. The Luminary responsible for the war, the same one carved into this podium. There's something mentioned about it here," he said, pointing out an image drawn on the scroll.

Their eyes traced the path of Arenius' outstretched finger until it settled on the depiction of a colossal reptile. Judging by the illustration, the creature dwarfed the Light Bringers standing nearby, easily surpassing them in size by fifteenfold. Its massive body resembled that of four armored war elephants melded together, while its seven sinuous necks soared far above the heads of the awestruck Light Bringers. Crowning its head were a series of horn-tipped protuberances arranged in a majestic circle.

"It says Herakles delivered the final blow which banished Izraga to the Nether."

"If this Izraga was defeated, how can it be responsible for the continuous demon presences?" Cornelius asked.

"Maybe, it's trying to return somehow," Floriana answered.

"Listen to this, fire, blunt force to scaly body, exposed eyes are written as weaknesses beside it."

"That's not much. So let's try not to ever come across it," Floriana said.

"Well, if it has weaknesses, it can be defeated," Cornelius assured firmly.

"The scroll is a complete history for the Light Bringers, and this place was one of many places for the Light Bringers to train and take refuge. With the library built over it and the stairs enchanted, to keep demons out," Arenius continued excitedly, bristly tracing his finger in every direction along the scroll. His finger stopped at another point on the scroll. "The demons have gone as far as to kill Light Bringers, as a means to push back the Light Bringers unification."

"That explains why they've been hunting us relentlessly. It all makes sense now," Cornelius responded, backing away from the scroll.

"What makes sense?" Arenius and Floriana asked in unison.

"All of this! Augustus, his pursuit. Somehow, he knew the next Light Bringer would be awakening. This is why he started his push for power. Initiating the Praetorian Guard, to protect him, with wanting me to lead it. He just didn't expect my son to be the one to awaken. Neither did I," he relented, turning to face Arenius. "And if he continues to grow in power like he has, there's no telling what will become of the Republic. He needs to be stopped."

"How," Floriana questioned, a face full of doubt.

The room fell silent as the visualization came to them, where the world's ruling power was being governed by a demon.

Breaking the silence, "Uh, the sun will be rising soon," Cornelius said, "And we need to be out of here before it does. Let's take what time we have left and look around for anything useful," he suggested, leaving them standing at the podium.

"Your father is correct. It's best we see what else this place has to offer," Floriana said, prying Arenius away from the scroll to follow behind Cornelius to the training area below.

Accompanied by Floriana, Cornelius gracefully descended the ornate staircase to the right and was drawn instinctively towards the armory located at the back of the hall. As they walked, they passed shelves filled with ancient scrolls before reaching the bustling training pit. Lagging behind, Arenius paused to gaze at the meticulously crafted wooden training dummies, picturing in his mind's eye all the legendary Light Bringers who might have once honed their skills against them.

Having honed his expertise during extensive military service and enriched by voyages through diverse realms, Cornelius swiftly identified the ancient armor and weaponry based on subtle nuances unique to each kingdom. The supple leather herringbone straps intertwined with gleaming bronze scales unmistakably hailed from the Egyptian lands, while the vividly-hued sleeved tunic paired with a formidable iron breastplate bore the hallmark of Persia's legendary Immortals. A captivating array of historical armors and weapons adorned the room, meticulously preserved on headless mannequins, each piece a testament to its rich heritage and storied past.

"Arenius, over here," Cornelius called out, waving him over, his attention locked ahead of him.

"What is it Pa?"

Cornelius stood in silence, his gaze fixed on a distant point. Intrigued, Arenius followed Cornelius' line of sight, navigating through an array of gleaming body armor and an assortment of weapons meticulously arranged on racks. As he moved forward, the glint of sharpened blades and the dull gleam of blunt instruments caught his eye. After a brief pause, he stopped in front of a lone mannequin, mesmerized by the stunning suit of armor it wore—its intricate detailing and impeccable craftsmanship held him spellbound.

"This is amazing," Arenius admired with a whisper, raising a hand to touching the armor.

One of Rome's best designed armor, the Lorica Segmentata rested on the wooden mannequin. Each circular metal band was meticulously fastened to supple leather straps that hugged the spine snugly, while additional metal plates extended over his shoulders like protective wings, forming sturdy guards against any threat on the battlefield.

Arenius gazed at his mirrored image in the gleaming armor, its iron surface glinting like molten silver. He delicately ran his finger along the intricate design of a blazing sun, intricately carved into the upper shoulder plate.

"Appears to be a perfect match for you," Floriana said, assessing the armor, eye gauging the armor to Arenius size.

"It's fashioned in the design of *Lorica Segmentata*, but I don't know a blacksmith who could craft body armor so perfectly. There's not a single imperfection in its quality," Cornelius suggested, walking around Arenius to see the armor from every possible angle. "I can't think what it maybe, but there's something unique about this armor."

"What makes this really strange is knowing armor was never crafted for someone of my age. Where did it come from? Or why is there Roman armor here? If Rome knew of this, none of this would be here," Arenius continued.

"I agree. But does it really matter, with all you have seen? What you need to know is that there's well-crafted armor in front of you, and as your mother said, it seems to be your exact size. So, stop wasting time and try it on."

Assisted by his parents, Arenius swiftly donned and fastened the intricate armor. "*She was right again*," Arenius thought, seeing how the Lorica Segmentata perfectly fitted his youthful frame, as if it was specifically crafted for him.

"Look at you," Floriana took a step back, her gaze sweeping over him.

"How do I look?" Arenius asked, putting himself on display.

"Like a true Legionnaire," Cornelius added, saluting Arenius with a single pound of his chest. Arenius began to turn away.

"Arenius, I see you and I always have. I know I've been a difficult father, and I apologize for my ways. All I ever wanted was for you to be something great to the world."

"You're only saying that now because I have the power of a Light Bringer. Not because you actually believe in me, and who I was before," Arenius quipped.

"You're wrong son. I always believe in you. I was just trying to get you to believe in yourself, that's all. You were my son before and you are my son now, nothing can change that," Cornelius ended and turned away.

Arenius promptly grabbed him by the bicep, "It's ok, Pa, you did what you thought was right. And now I understand, it was meant to be. What matters now is that we are together and remain together," he affirmed, releasing his arm.

Cornelius cleared his throat, "With that being said it's about time we go. We don't want those soldiers waking while we're still down here."

"What's our next move?" Floriana asked, adjusting Arenius' cloak, then his hair.

"First thing, how we go and find an Inn, eat and rest. And in that order. It's been weeks since we slept in a comfortable bed. Afterward, I say we find the first ship out of here to Tarsus. Once there we have enough coin to do whatever we like."

"Tarsus? I can't go there, I told you," Arenius chimed in

"No, your exact words were, you needed to go to Alexandria. We fulfilled that, now there's nothing else. It seems you found what you needed to know, right? Unless you had more visions?"

"No," Arenius answered, unsure of what else to say.

"Then its final, Tarsus it is. There you can figure out what you are supposed to do next, and I promise we'll support the best way we can. But first we simply need to get out of Augustus' reach."

"I hear both of you," Floriana chimed in, "Whatever we do, it can be discussed over a meal."

After briefly locking eyes with his father, Arenius broke away and headed for the exit. Being honest with himself, he currently was not sure what his next move should be. He had not heard from the Divine Speaker since receiving the gladius nor had he had a vision guiding to the next objective. He was simply on his own, to walk his chosen path, glancing back at his parents maybe not truly alone. Either way he was quickly learning being a Light Bringer was not as clear cut as he had expected.

"Thanks for the help, love," Cornelius added, facing Floriana.

"Well, I figure I should jump in and save you before you say something you'll regret. But I want you to keep in mind, he's trying to figure out this whole thing. I can't imagine being in his position right now. I need you to know that," Moving back from the stash of body armor, she halted abruptly as a new discovery seized her focus.

"What is it?" Cornelius asked.

"Nothing. I see something I want to check out before we leave. Go ahead, I'll catch up."

"You sure?"

"Yes, I'll right behind you."

Cornelius gave a curt nod, "Make it quick," he muttered before pivoting away. He strode past the bustling training pit and ascended the worn stone steps leading to the exit.

"Where is mom?" Arenius questioned, seeing Cornelius reach the podium's platform alone.

"She's right behind," Cornelius answered, coming to Arenius side while he was further studying the Light Bringer scroll one last time.

XVII

A tense hush enveloped the corridor as Arenius and Cornelius stood braced against the walls flanking the staircase, anticipating Floriana's reappearance. Despite their proximity of mere feet, the emotional chasm between them might as well have spanned a vast distance, leaving Arenius feeling isolated and distant from his companion.

"Can I ask you a question?" Arenius felt the weight of the awkward silence pressing down on them, prompting him to speak up and break the tension.

Cornelius stole a quick look back in the direction he left Floriana, "Appears we have time," he said seeing the steps clear.

"Do you really believe we can stop Augustus?"

"At this point with all the restructuring he is doing, it's going to be nearly impossible to get near him. So no, but that doesn't mean we shouldn't try. Especially if what the Divine Speaker says is true."

"Look at that, both of my strong men, waiting for me," Floriana interrupted, upon reaching the platform, a new bow in her hand and quiver full of arrows across her back.

"I see you found a new toy," Arenius said as he approached her, and seeing her equipment.

"It was on a wall back there. I figured nobody was going to

miss it. Maybe it will come in handy against the demons."

"You do remember I can only send them back to Nether?" Arenius questioned.

"Yes, I do, but that doesn't mean I can't make their life here a painful one," she smirked, raising the bow to pull back on the string to display its tautness.

Clasped in her hands was a recurve bow crafted from the resilient acacia tree that grew only in the hidden valleys of the realm. The bow's sinewy curves mimicked the formidable horns of a charging bull, exuding an aura of primal strength. Its ebony wood bore intricate patterns of gleaming gold and silver that seemed to cascade like molten streams of precious metals from the bow's hilt, tracing a mesmerizing path along its supple limbs until culminating in a fiery burst at its tip. Despite its ornate appearance, the bow remained remarkably light, enabling swift and agile movements without compromising on its sheer power or deadly accuracy. This was no ordinary weapon; it was a masterpiece coveted by archers far and wide, whispered about in hushed tones as the ultimate instrument of precision and prowess.

"What's that written on the grip?" Arenius asked, as he admired the weapon's craftsmanship.

"I don't know. I thought those lines were part of the design," Floriana responded.

Arenius squinted as he brought the bow's grip closer, reading the small glyphs, "*Banisher of Seth*," he murmured.

"The Banisher, I like that," Floriana said, admiring the weapon's design.

"Who's Seth?" Cornelius questioned.

"I read about Seth in the scroll, it was one of the first demons that tried to take control of Egypt long ago but was banished to the Nether before it could succeed. Where did you find this?" Arenius continued.

"It was on a wall back there. When I saw it, I was immediately drawn to it. Felt as though I needed to have it," she answered.

"If you felt the need to have it, I'm glad you took it. If there's anyone I want with a bow in their hands at my side, it's you," Cornelius reassured. Facing Arenius, "Your mother is the best archer I have ever come across."

"I know, she told me. Were you guys ever planning to tell me where Ma from or did being a Roman outweigh that as well?"

Cornelius and Floriana sighed and shrug.

"Never mind," Arenius retracted annoyingly, turned and headed up the spiral staircase to the library.

Yanking on a weathered oak lever nestled in a recess hewn into the ancient stone wall, the massive shelf groaned open once more. A slender beam of sunlight spilled into the dim stairwell from the hidden library, gradually widening with each metallic clank. Only after the shelf had fully swung open and their vision adjusted to the sudden brightness, did they discern four Praetorian soldiers stationed a few paces away from the chamber's threshold. Each soldier was strikingly identical in stature, clad in impeccably crafted obsidian armor that bore the unmistakable insignia of their legion, their gazes veiled beneath the shadowy brims of their helmets.

Arenius's sword slid smoothly out of its scabbard with a faint metallic whisper, as he shifted into a practiced battle stance. Not far behind, Cornelius mirrored his movements with a fluid grace, his eyes focused and alert. Meanwhile, Floriana's fingers moved deftly as she notched an arrow onto her bowstring, her gaze unwavering as she honed in on her target.

"We were wondering how long you were going to fiddle around

dhow there," shouted one of the soldiers, stepping out from the other three.

"I would ask what you wanted, but I believe I am aware," Arenius barked, gripping his weapon tighter.

"So, you are the Light Bringer. Much smaller than I had imagined, especially for being the one responsible of banishing so many of the emperor's finest soldiers to the Nether. But what do I know? Your knowledge is passed on from one Light Bringer to the next. There's centuries of knowledge in that human brain of yours, am I right?" the soldier continued. "Maybe the Praetorian are not up to par just yet."

"If you value your dark soul, I suggest you leave now," Cornelius ordered.

Cutting his eyes to Cornelius, "I can't do that, and neither can you," the soldier responded. "An incantation has been spoken over the entrance; therefore, it will remain closed until the sun rises. Giving us plenty of time to deal with you. And you, general, how the mighty have fallen. Did you think by freeing the old hag, we would lose you? Know that we will hunt you until Izraga's purpose is fulfilled, for we have eyes everywhere. And your childish against Augustus' cause is of little concern. Because once we get you back to Rome, our priest will have you singing in tune in no time."

"Your souls will exit your bodies before I allow you to lay a hand on my father," Arenius growled through clenched teeth.

"Well, let's see how good your tune is, Light Bringer," he ended, promptly stepping back in line.

Furious flames of rage consumed Arenius as he faced the relentless demons that plagued his family. While he knew his fate was intertwined with battling these malevolent forces indefinitely, his immediate concern was shielding his parents from harm. Determined to bring an end to the torment and secure his family's safety permanently, he steeled himself for the impending confrontation.

The Vestas watched as the Praetorian Guards raised their hands and tilted their heads in unison, their voices merging in a harmonious chant.

"Unum Preco Regenerationein Tenebrae Tuae," (One night will herald regeneration), they repeated.

"What is this, Arenius? Why are they saying that?" Cornelius asked, while keeping his eyes locked on the guards.

"I'm not sure," Arenius answered.

"Whatever is happening, it can't be good," Floriana added.

Ensnared in their hypnotic state, the Praetorians' bodies convulsed violently, yet their relentless incantations persisted.

"You guys will not believe what I am seeing," Arenius said.

"If you're talking about the black smoke emanating from their bodies. I see it," Floriana said, staring at the bizarre event.

They watched on as smoke poured from their eyes, mouth, and chest as though a fire was raging within them.

"Not this again," Arenius thought, reflecting back on his first experience with demons at the House of Augustus.

The dense, ebony smoke loomed ominously over the Praetorians' heads like a malevolent thundercloud. Arenius sensed a churning in his gut, a sensation long forgotten since they set off on their journey - fear. Determined to intervene, he knew that unless he halted the unfolding events, his parents would not see the light of another day.

Clutching the polished ivory handle of his gladius with knuckles turning white, Arenius surged ahead with a lightning-like swiftness that momentarily stunned his parents. His gaze locked onto the unsuspecting soldier who had dared to confront them, and with a swift motion, he raised his blade in a menacing arc. His singular objective was to cleave through the air and strike at the soldier's neck, envisioning a mesmerizing spectacle where the head would disintegrate into shimmering particles of light before the bewildered eyes of the remaining three soldiers.

In his mind, every step taken felt like wading through thick honey, each movement deliberate and heavy. As he closed the gap between them, the air crackled with anticipation. With a swift and fluid motion, Arenius arced his blade towards his adversary, the steel glinting in the dim light as it sliced through the space between them. At the brink of impact, the enemy's face twisted into a sinister grin, their eyes locking onto Arenius with an unsettling gaze.

Instead of meeting flesh, blood, and bone, Arenius's strike met an invisible wall that reverberated with a powerful energy. The force of the barrier hurled him across the chamber, crashing through a towering shelf laden with ancient scrolls. The wooden structure shattered upon contact, sending splinters and parchment flying in all directions like a chaotic storm. Finally coming to rest amidst the debris-laden floor, Arenius lay still as remnants of shattered history rained down around him.

"Arenius," Cornelius shouted, taking off after his son.

Floriana followed suite and darted after him, her heart pounding as she drew a pair of sleek arrows from her leather quiver. With precision honed through countless hours of practice, she sighted the soldiers, her fingers deftly releasing the arrows in quick succession from the polished bow that gleamed in the dim light. The arrows flew forth, meeting the same unseen force and sent them ricocheting off in unexpected trajectories. Each impact against the invisible barrier created mesmerizing ripples resembling liquid silver dancing across its surface. As the last ripple faded into stillness, the barrier dissolved into thin air, vanishing without a trace as if it had never existed at all.

"Arenius, are you ok?" Cornelius asked upon reaching him. He promptly brushed aside the debris covering him, to find Arenius gasping for breath, blood oozing from his mouth. With a sigh of relief, "What in Jupiter's name were you thinking, advancing like that?"

"Your father's right, and if we didn't have other concerns, I would've used one of these arrows on you. That was just reckless," Floriana added, kneeling at their side.

"I instructed you to be patient, and wait for the enemy to make a move, find the cracks in their defense first, then strike," Cornelius said, sitting Arenius up.

"In the moment it felt right," Arenius responded, wincing at the pain, his body feeling as though it was being pricked by thousands of hot needles.

"What about now?" Floriana continued, not taking her eyes off the Praetorian soldiers.

"I think we need a different approach," Arenius replied as Cornelius hoisted him to his feet.

"You bet we do," Cornelius nodded in agreement without hesitation.

"Well, when you two find that approach let me know," Floriana said, her attention still locked on the soldiers, an arrow notched and ready for release.

Standing together, the Vestas begin to witness a mesmerizing transformation. The billowing smoke that had formed over the soldiers had begun morphed into a swirling vortex, reaching ten feet in height. As the four soldiers crumpled to the ground, wisps of smoke continued to slither out of their unmoving forms, fueling the spiraling anomaly. Violent gusts of wind whipped through the library, compelling the Vestas to shield their eyes from the chaos unfolding before them. Loose objects within the rotunda were flung perilously around by the tempestuous currents. Then, like a cascade of rushing water, the vortex suddenly imploded upon itself, converging into a singular point at its core.

After enduring the tumultuous storm, the fierce winds gradually subsided, carrying away the final traces of smoke clinging to the Praetorians' lifeless forms. Suddenly, a pitch-black orb materialized, merging with the air in a haunting spectacle. In an instant, the orb swelled into a blazing cone of flames and billowing smoke, only to implode upon itself, birthing a vortex that tore through the very fabric of reality before them. No explanations were necessary as they gazed at the mesmerizing portal, their apprehension mounting as they pondered what malevolent entity might emerge. Their primary concern lingered on whether they possessed the means to thwart this impending threat.

The atmosphere transformed, thickening into an oppressive weight as the portal rumbled ominously. A palpable malevolence radiated from the entrance to the Nether, sending shivers down their spines. From within the portal emerged a colossal foot with three menacing toes, each tipped with razor-sharp talons that gouged deep into the marble floor. The foot and shin were encased in iridescent avian scales, giving way to knees that bent backwards unnaturally. As more of these demonic beings emerged, its body cloaked in sleek owl feathers, boasting expansive wings that unfurled majestically from their backs.

Arenius' blade continued to shine brightly as the beast emerged entirely from the shimmering portal.

"What is that?" Arenius said, his eyes widening as he studied its spindly body.

"Your grandfather called them Strix. But they were simply fables to keep children in line with tales of ill omens told by elders."

"That's no tale," Floriana mumbled, unconsciously taking a step back but keeping her bows aimed at the creature.

The shimmering portal released the creature into full view, revealing the apex beast towering at its true height of seven feet. Its hands mirrored its feet with sharp talons on three elongated fingers. A deep and narrow chest was concealed under matted gray fur. Antlers gracefully extended from each side of its owl-like face.

Having passed through the portal, the Strix's head twisted on its sinuous neck, pinpointing their presence. "There you go," its shrill voice echoed off the stone walls, while the portal's thick smoke began to break into wisps and dissipate in thin air. "Oh, how great it feels to be ins this realm."

XVIII

Arenius found it bizarre to witness a bird fluently conversing in their language.

"How is this possible?" Cornelius asked as if read Areius' mind.

"I see me talking confuses your mortal minds. My kind speaks every language in your realm and more. We have become more than The One could dream of," The Strix's eyes, resembling the golden orbs of a hunting panther, as she addressed Arenius.

"Too bad it won't help you," Arenius said confidently.

"You want to skip pleasantries, fine, I'm here to extinguish your feeble existence, and drag your father back. Let me warn you, I'm not as easily defeated as my lesser counterparts. I can remain here in your world as long as I need to fulfill the emperor's...."

Mid-sentence, the creature's words faded into a guttural growl as Floriana's fingers released the tensioned bowstring. The arrow sliced through the air, aiming unerringly for the spot where she imagined its heart beat beneath the monstrous exterior.

The Strix unleashed a piercing scream that reverberated through the library, causing them to instinctively shield their ears. Floriana managed to release another arrow before the deafening sound wave hit, halting her projectile in its tracks. For a fleeting moment, the arrow hung suspended in mid-air before gravity reclaimed it, sending it tumbling to the ground moments later.

"Pathetic mortal, believing your predictable attacks could stop a ranking Luminary such as myself," the Strix continued, after they had removed their hands from their ears. "But being you're eager to fight, so be it."

With a thunderous beat of its wings, the Strix lunged forward, its razor-sharp talons poised to ensnare its unsuspecting victim. It closed the vast thirty-foot distance between them in a heartbeat. Just as the creature was about to seize its prey, Arenius plummeted towards his parents, forcefully propelling them out of harm's way. In a swift and heart-stopping moment, the beast's talons snatched him from the air. The violent impact caused him to involuntarily release his gladius, sending it tumbling towards the ground.

"*Arenius*," Floriana screamed as he was carried away.

Rapidly spiraling, the Strix relentlessly hoisted Arenius high above the rotunda floor, its talons gripping his body tightly. Were it not for the sturdy armor he had appropriated from the Light Bringer chamber, he was convinced his ribs would have splintered under the pressure. The ceaseless spiral and sudden jerks induced a queasy sensation in Arenius, battling against waves of nausea threatening to overwhelm him.

The searing agony ripped through him as he crashed into the towering shelves of ancient scrolls in the library's upper levels. Each impact sent tremors of pain through his body, the wooden shelves groaning in protest as they gave way to his force. Without The One's protective energy coursing through him, Arenius would have become a morbid painting, leaving a crimson trail on the pristine walls of knowledge. Ignoring the throbbing ache that threatened to overwhelm him, Arenius knew that reclaiming his gladius was imperative if he wished to survive the imminent battle ahead.

Bracing for the imminent four shelves hurtling towards him, a sharp projectile whizzed past, narrowly avoiding his face before embedding itself in the Strix's armpit. With a piercing cry of agony, the demon let go of Arenius who plummeted ten feet, crashing onto the second tier of shelves and tumbling down to meet the unforgiving embrace of the icy marble floor below.

The arrow found its mark, but it failed to incapacitate the powerful demon. Without faltering in its airborne movement, the Strix forcefully removed the arrow lodged beneath its wing with its enormous claws, inspecting the sharp, jagged point of the projectile.

"How can a mere mortal hurt me?" the Strix shrieked, tossing the projectile aside. "How dare you insult me with such meager things," it continued searching below for the one responsible, zeroing it's gaze on Cornelius and Floriana. "I see, the bow of Horus," it recited, seeing Floriana preparing another arrow to release. "You're not worthy of sending me back to the Nether, neither is your son," he cackled with a maniacal caw.

"Maybe so, but apparently I'm worthy enough to cause you a hell of a lot of pain."

Quivering with fury, the Strix sleekly folded its wings against its sleek body, hurtling towards its prey with lethal intent. Cornelius and Floriana stood firm as the creature rapidly approached, unfurling its massive wings to slow its descent while extending its formidable talons forward. Just as the beast was about to ensnare them, Floriana unleashed her arrow, piercing the creature's chest with precision. In a synchronized move, she and Cornelius swiftly dodged aside as the Strix crashed onto the ground with a thunderous impact, carving out a deep crater in the marble floor and leaving a trail of shattered tiles in its wake where they had just been.

Without hesitation, Cornelius sprinted towards the monstrous creature as it lay sprawled on the ground, his weapon poised high above his head. With a swift motion, he aimed to strike at the beast's skull. However, the sharp edge of his gladius abruptly halted upon meeting the Strix's impenetrable hide, akin to trying to pierce through solid rock.

Puzzled, Cornelius examined his blade, "What is-"

Without warning, the Strix's eyes shot open with a piercing intensity. In a swift motion, it delivered a powerful backhand to Cornelius, propelling him through the air. He soared fifteen feet before crashing into a stone column, his body crumpling in unconsciousness upon impact.

"No," Floriana's anguished cry filled the air as she unleashed a swift barrage of arrows towards the menacing demon, her heart wrenching at the sight of her husband lying motionless on the cold ground.

The Strix rose with deliberate grace, unfurling a majestic wing to shield its face. With each arrow piercing its flesh, a shudder rippled through its formidable frame.

"How feisty have humans become. All emotion, no bite. Haven't you learned no matter what weapon you wield, it won't be enough to bring me down," the Strix hawked, dashing towards them closing the distance once more.

Darting swiftly, Floriana maneuvered through the chaos to kneel by Cornelius, unleashing arrows with precision until the quiver ran dry. The Strix agilely evaded most of her shots, but some found their mark, drawing blood. Undeterred, the creature closed in on them, its imposing figure casting a shadow over Floriana. Sensing impending danger, she pulled Cornelius close, bracing for the imminent end.

"You fought, how should I say it?" he taunted, removing arrows from its wing and licking away the blood, "Your best," it taunted.

"What are you?" Floriana demanded, embracing her husband tighter.

"I'm one of many. The One failed to see greatness in us. But instead, The One chooses you, humans, the weaker vessel of all creation, to be the possessor of this world. No more. I promise to be a little merciful," the Strix shrieked, pulling the remaining arrows free, letting them drop at its feet as its wounds began stitching back together. "I'll be nice enough to kill you before your husband awakes. And when he does, he will not even remember he had a family."

"Do what you must, but you will never get your hands on my husband or my son," she blared, removing a small dagger from beneath her tunic.

"I beg to differ, but we can discuss it more in the Nether," lifting its talons to strike.

"Get away from them," shouted a voice from above, when from a high shelf Arenius descended, holding his gladius up, and plunged his blade deep between the creature's shoulder blade, driving the Strix down to its knees.

"What are you waiting for?" Arenius questioned standing on the creature's back, the sword still embedded. "Get him back into the chamber below, you'll be safe there," he ended as the Strix shrieked in pain.

"I can't leave-"

"Go, now," he bellowed.

"Then take this," she offered, tossing the Bow of Horus to Arenius, then promptly stood, dropping the quiver to drag Cornelius by his armor back towards the Light Bringer chamber entrance.

Balancing the weight of the gladius in his grasp, Arenius clutched the handle tightly, the blade buried deep in the Strix's back. With a swift motion, he snatched the bow, fastening it securely across his chest. In response, the Strix recovered from its momentary daze and thrashed wildly, its talons reaching menacingly towards Arenius. Anticipating its every move, he skillfully evaded each slashing attack by swiftly swaying from side to side, mirroring the creature's deadly dance.

Arenius had initially aimed the gleaming blade at the creature's head, but as he shifted to target Floriana, the beast swiftly altered its position. Writhing in agony, the monstrous being thrashed its massive body against shelves, with each impact akin to a charging war chariot. And despite the violent onslaught, Arenius clung on tenaciously. An ethereal energy enveloped him, instilling a newfound sense of mastery over the chaotic encounter brought by the arrival of the Strix.

Mounted on the back of the Strix with a fierce grip akin to a wild boar's, Arenius taunted, "Dislike being under human command? Stay clear of my realm then," as he forcefully drove the blade in further.

"If it's a ride you want boy, then you shall have it," the Strix replied, stretching out its massive wings.

With powerful, deliberate movements, the Strix propelled itself upwards, leaping with a force that defied gravity. Despite his precarious position, Arenius clung on tenaciously, his fingers tightly gripping a solitary beam suspended high above the ground. As the Strix's wings beat rhythmically, each stroke lifted them both further into the sky.

In a heartbeat, he ascended swiftly until he could almost reach out and touch the gleaming orb suspended above the grand rotunda. Despite his perilous situation, Arenius couldn't deny the awe-inspiring magnificence of the sphere at close range. Yet, before he could revel in its splendor, a sudden jolt shook him back to reality as the Strix plummeted into a dizzying descent.

Arenius marveled at the mind-bending velocity, his disbelief melting away as the rush of wind tousled his hair. The urge to leap surged within him, only to be quashed by the terrify-ing prospect of a bone-jarring collision with the earth below. Clinging on with gritted teeth, he braced himself against the tumultuous spin of his surroundings, fixating his gaze on a single point on the ground beneath him, preparing for the impending impact.

Twenty feet...Fifteen feet...Ten feet...

As doubt crept in, the Strix veered sharply in the opposite direction, yanking upwards. The sudden maneuver wrenched Arenius' blade from the Strix's hide. Dislodged, the blade sent Arenius careening headlong down a narrow aisle. Amidst the chaotic descent, a symphony of cracks echoed as he tumbled uncontrollably before finally skidding to a stop on his back.

"This can't be my-"

Mid-sentence, his eyes locked onto the Strix plunging down for its lethal strike. With lightning reflexes, he twisted away just in time, witnessing the beast's razor-sharp talons shatter the marble beneath into a cloud of fine powder. Arenius swiftly darted through the labyrinth of aisles, strategically weaving be-tween shelves to shield himself, disrupting the Strix's predatory focus with each elusive maneuver.

"There's nothing you can do to escape your death, Light

Bringer," the Strix laughed, taking flight once more.

"You believe this is me running?" Arenius quipped, being sure to keep his head low. "Oh, how you are mistaken. If anything, this is me allowing you to believe you have a chance," Arenius ended, promptly pressing his body tight against the shelving as the Strix's shadow passed overhead.

"Believe me when I say you're no hero, boy. Nothing about you speaks hero, before recent events you lived in the shadow of your father. And even now you have the false belief that you can somehow save yourself or your parents," the Strix squawked, orbiting the golden sphere, which gave it a perfect view of the rotunda.

"If I'm no hero, then why are you here?" he finished, stopping at the end of an aisle, peeking out from the corner, scanning for his attacker. Although his sword continued to glow intensely, he found nothing but silence and flickering shadows from the burning brazier. "Where are you?" he whispered to himself, his eyes darting in all directions.

A soft breeze caressed his skin from the ceiling, prompting Arenius to instinctively somersault away from the ledge. The air was suddenly filled with feathers resembling arrowhead, piercing through the space where he had stood mere moments before.

Rolling to a shaky stand, a surge of agony shot through his shoulder. Investigating the source, he discovered an iridescent seven-inch feather embedded in his flesh of his arm. The feather's texture resembled that of Roman steel unyielding and cool against his fingers. With a grimace, he extracted it from his skin, feeling the sickening pull as blood welled up around the wound. The feather dropped to the ground with a soft thud. Ripping a strip of fabric from his tunic, he pressed it against the injury, staunching the crimson flow with deliberate care.

This has to do for now, he thought studying his wound.

Refusing to linger in any single spot, he propelled himself forward at a breakneck pace. The gentle caress of the breeze brushed against his skin just moments before a flurry of feathers whizzed past him, reminiscent of a swarm of arrows blotting out the sky. Dodging sharply to the right, then swiftly veering left, Arenius strained every sinew to maintain distance between himself and the Strix's unrelenting onslaught. Like Theseus navigating the intricate twists of the Labyrinth while hunted by the Minotaur, Arenius found himself pursued relentlessly through every corner of the library.

"What's wrong, Vir? Were you planning to dispatch me easily?" the Strix teased, hovering high in the rotunda.

Coming to a sudden halt, under the cover of a towering book-case, "I'm not even breaking a sweat, you oversized parrot," Arenius heckled, while remaining out of sight. "My father's training was more challenging than this."

"Your pathetic excuse at slandering is meaningless," the Strix said with a shrill laugh. "How I miss the thrill of the chase. The thought of me drinking down your warm blood is truly invigorating," the Strix continued, shivering in anticipation, causing several feathers to shake loose from its body. "Do you not know your very existence is worthless. Nothing you do will change the outcome. Izraga will bring the human world to ruin and submission with fire and brimstone. Stomping the life out of every Light Bringer who challenges his will."

"Keep chirping, bird," Arenius thought, while weaving his way through the library's many aisles.

Successfully engaging the Strix in conversation, he navigated the rotunda until he reached the spot where Cornelius had collapsed. There, lying on the ground, was Floriana's distinctive quiver. The sight triggered a flood of memories, bringing back Cornelius poignant words to him. *"Your weapon is an extension of you, lose it, you lose a piece of you."*

Maintaining a cautious distance, the Strix hindered Arenius from effectively engaging in combat. Survival in this skirmish hinged on his skill to tip the scales in his favor. Securing those elusive arrows became paramount for him to gain an edge and turn the tide of battle in his favor.

Arenius raced at full speed, his heart pounding in sync with his thundering footsteps as he outpaced the relentless Strix's barrage. The air filled with the sound of sharp feathers whistling past him, drawing nearer with each attack. As he rounded a corner, his gaze locked onto the gleaming quiver resting just a stone's throw away behind a towering pillar. With determination blazing in his eyes, he lunged towards it, narrowly evading a deadly storm of razor-edged feathers that tore into the solid marble column where he had stood just moments before.

After the chaotic rush subsided, Arenius's hand cautiously closed around the quiver. His heart sank as he discovered it devoid of any arrows, rendering it useless in his current predicament. A flicker of disbelief crossed his face before he nonchalantly released his grip, allowing the empty quiver to tumble to the ground at his feet.

"What is it boy? Did mommy use up all you precious arrows," the Strix teased, sending another blast of feathers, to pelting Arenius' cover.

After running throughout the entire library and back to where he had starred, he had nothing to show for it. No means to fight at a distance. There was nothing he could do to protect himself or his parents.

"The power is within," Arenius perked up as a voice he recognized broke the silence. Quickly scanning his surroundings, he found himself still alone. *"The power is within."*

Arenius's awareness sharpened as he discerned the voice resonating not around him, but deep within his core. His senses tingled with a familiar curiosity, reminiscent of his initial revelation at the sacred temple. With a fluid motion, he unslung the bow from his back, and a primal instinct guided his hand to caress the taut string. The instant his fingertips grazed the bowstring, a symphony of colors burst forth, enveloping the bow in a mesmerizing display of shimmering aquamarine lights that seemed to dance in harmony with its awakening spirit.

As he tugged the string tighter, a shimmering arrow of pure light took shape, poised for release.

"By The One," Arenius mouthed in awe.

"Come boy."

Emerging swiftly from concealment, his bow poised high and the string taut mere inches from his keen eye, he directed his aim towards the spot where the Strix had vanished. The Strix, swirling overhead akin to hungry vultures homing in on a fresh kill, spotted the glint of light seeping through the cracks behind the ancient pillar and swiftly plummeted towards his concealed position. Arenius maintained a serene composure, honing his focus to regulate his breaths as he meticulously aligned the arrowhead with his elusive target, biding his time with unwavering patience.

Arenius strained against the arrow, muscles taut as the Strix dove towards him in a deadly descent. Years of watching predatory birds taught him their tactic: waiting until the last moment to strike with their razor-sharp talons. Anticipation gripped him as he wagered that this demon-born creature operated similarly. His hypothesis proved true as the Strix hurtled closer, its speed diminishing only slightly before its claws tore through his vulnerable skin.

In a suspended moment, Arenius felt time slow as he continued to grip his mother's sleek bow, its polished wood cool against his palm. His father's teachings echoed in his mind, transforming him from prey to predator. Focused on the Strix before him, its chest bare and vulnerable, he eased his fingers from the taut bowstring. The arrow, shimmering with an otherworldly glow, sliced through the air with a sharp whistle, hurtling towards its mark. Its luminous aura pulsed brighter and brighter until it exploded into a searing brilliance, surging forward with unstoppable force.

The Strix reeled with its wings flailing to shield its sensitive eyes from the blinding burst of light hurtling towards it. Without a moment to counter, the arrow found its mark with precision, burying deep into the creature's chest. The impact jolted the Strix in mid-flight, sending it hurtling backwards towards the vaulted ceiling, where it was skewered onto the radiant golden orb of Thoth.

Impaled on the orb, the monstrous creature let out a piercing scream and contorted in agony. Arenius confidently notched another arrow, conjuring it into existence, and fixed his gaze on the rope tethering the orb. With a steady hand, he released the arrow, hitting its mark with precision, causing the entire contraption to plummet down, crushing the Strix into the searing brazier below. A cloud of smoke and singed feathers billowed out in every direction. As the debris settled, Arenius unsheathed his blade and approached the fallen beast cautiously.

"You think by sending me back to the Nether, your battle has ended?" the Strix wheezed, buried beneath the weight of the sphere. "I think not, boy, your fight has just begun. Izraga will have his way," he claimed, watching Arenius raise his gladius. "Send me to the Nether and a legion will come forth as the rushing sea," he laughed.

"Then I'll be waiting. And give your Augustus a message. No matter how far he goes or how long it takes, he will meet my blade. He should have never threatened my family," With a swift and precise strike, Arenius brought down his sword, cleanly severing the Strix's head from its body, silencing its eerie laughter in an eerie instant.

XIX

The great Library of Alexandria lay silent once more. The echoes of the battle had faded, leaving only the faint crackle of dying embers and the scent of ash that clung to the air like a ghost of what had transpired. Shattered scrolls littered the marble floors, their edges blackened where fire and shadow had wrestled for dominion.

Arenius stood in the heart of the devastation, his chest heaving, the last shimmer of the Strix's fading into nothing. The demon's shriek still trembled in his ears, a whisper of a victory hard-won. He gripped his still-gleaming sword for a moment longer before gradually sliding it into its silver sheath, where it hung heavy at his side, its once-radiant blade fading to dull lifelessness.

"I'm going to sleep for a week," he murmured.

He drew a long breath, forcing the tension from his body. The air was thick, almost sacred.

He turned and began to move—limping slightly—through the ruined corridors toward the hidden chamber beneath the library. His mother's bow was in his hand, the curve of the polished yew still warm from the fight.

Down the spiral stairs, through the narrow passage of stone and dust, he found them.

Near the large podium Floriana was kneeling beside Cornelius, whose form lay sprawled on the cold floor. Her golden hair was loose from its braids, her face streaked with warrior's tears. She looked up sharply as Arenius entered, and the fear in her eyes melted into relief.

"Arenius!" she breathed, rising to her feet. "You're—by the gods, you're alive."

He gave a small nod, his voice rough. "I am. It's done, Mother."

He crossed the room and knelt beside his father. Cornelius's eyes fluttered open at the sound of his son's voice. His face was pale, marked with dust and a smear of blood at the temple. Arenius slid an arm under his shoulders, helping him to sit.

"Easy, Pa," he said softly. "You took quite the blow."

Cornelius groaned, blinking into focus. "The demon...? The creature—"

"Gone," Arenius answered. "The Strix won't plague us again."

Floriana pressed a trembling but firm hand to his shoulders, eyes glistening. "You faced it alone and came out on top," giving a faint smile.

"I had to," he said simply, looking into her eyes. "There wasn't time. I couldn't allow it to—"

"We know why you had to do it son. And I'm glad it was you who protected us," Cornelius said weakly.

For a long moment, the three of them said nothing. Only the faint crackle from the chamber's burning brazier, the sound of the world resettling after the storm.

Then Floriana reached out, her hand brushing her son's cheek. "You've grown beyond us, my son. You fight as if the gods themselves guide your hand."

Arenius shook his head. "The gods didn't save me. You did. With One's power, you both taught me to stand."

Cornelius bowed his head, shame flickering across his tired features. "And I failed you, Arenius."

Arenius frowned. "Father—"

"No," Cornelius said, his voice low but steady. "I doubted you. I doubted your strength, your visions, your purpose. I thought them the fancies of a boy. And yet it was you who stood against the darkness when I could not even stand on my own feet."

Arenius hesitated, the weight of those words pressing between them.

"You believed in reason, you fought for what you were trained to do," Arenius said softly. "I can't fault you for that. If not for your training, I sure would've fell to the demon. But sometimes... the world is darker than reason allows."

Cornelius gave a broken laugh. "Then it is time I learned to see through your eyes."

He reached for Arenius's hand and gripped it firmly, his old soldier fingers still calloused from years of battle. "From this day, I swear, my son, your mother and I will stand beside you. Whatever demons remain in this world, we will face them together, as a family."

Floriana placed her hand atop theirs. "By the light of the dawn and the memory of what we've lost, we vow it."

Arenius looked from one to the other, his father's proud, worn face, his mother's steady gaze, and for the first time since he had drawn his blade, he allowed himself to smile. A small, weary smile, but one born of peace.

"Then together," he said, "we will finish what has begun."

The light in the chamber began to shift as the first rays of dawn broke through, piercing the darkness in stairwell. The dust in the air glimmered gold.

Cornelius rose slowly, with Arenius and Floriana on either side of him. The three stood—not as warriors or scholars or hunters, but as something older and stronger: a family reborn in the ashes of battle.

"Come," Floriana said softly. "Before the librarians return. Let this place rest."

They ascended the winding stone stairwell, their footsteps echoing softly. When they reached the main hall, the devastation of the library spread before them, rows of toppled shelves, columns cracked, and the faint smell of burned ink.

Arenius paused at the threshold. He turned back once more, eyes sweeping across the grand chamber. "May its knowledge survive," he murmured.

Cornelius nodded. "Knowledge will endure. So long as there are those willing to defend it."

Together, they stepped out into the morning light. The city beyond the library's marble gates was still quiet—Alexandria awakening to another day, unaware that the battle between worlds had just been waged in its heart.

The sun climbed higher, spilling its warmth across the marble steps. Floriana adjusted her bow over her shoulder. Cornelius drew his cloak tight. Arenius stood between them, the young warrior who had looked into darkness and found the strength to return.

As they descended toward the city streets, a breeze stirred the ashes behind them.

The war was far from over. There was still a self-proclaimed emperor, possessed by a demon, that needed to be dealt with.

But Arenius no longer faced it alone.

Epilogue

February 2, 15 AD: Tarsus, Cilicia

In the distant outskirts of the sprawling Roman Empire, under a canopy of cloudless skies, a mysterious figure clad in a weathered cloak traverses a rugged pathway. The soles of their sandals bear the marks of an arduous journey across vast stretches of land. Their ultimate destination is a solitary villa perched atop a hill, framed by towering mountains in the distance. A single satchel swings from their sturdy shoulder, every footfall calculated and purposeful amidst fields of undulating lavender swaying gently in the breeze. As if guided by an unspoken connection to nature, they extend their hand and caress the velvety petals of the fragrant purple blooms.

Arriving at the villa's porch, they were greeted by a serene silence enveloping the humble abode. The encroaching vines and tangled weeds snaking up the walls whispered stories of neglect and abandonment, hinting at the long absence of its inhabitants. Despite its faded grandeur, the villa stood sturdy and proud, bearing witness to a bygone era when the vineyard flourished in abundance.

With a gentle nudge, the sturdy front door swung open, its creak reverberating through the silent house. Inside, every detail was immaculate; furniture arranged meticulously, frescoes vibrant and untouched by time. Standing in the doorway, the figure breathed in the familiar scent of the home, memories flooding back with each inhale. As they shut the door softly, they shed their cloak, letting the dim light dance off their gleaming Lorica Segmentata armor. Slowly unclasping their sheath, they lowered their sword with an ivory hilt to rest gracefully on the polished floorboards.

Moving purposefully towards the rear of the opulent villa, they reached a towering, robust bookcase brimming with an assortment of aged scrolls and parchments. With determined strength, they pushed the heavy shelf aside, unveiling a hidden chamber beyond. Stepping into the narrow enclosure, they gracefully sank to their knees. Their fingers traced the rough surface of the floor until they found the cool touch of an oil lamp nearby. Retrieving an iron rod and flint stone from their pocket, they expertly struck them together, igniting a warm flame within the lamp. The soft glow bathed the cramped space in a gentle orange light, exposing a meticulously carved four-foot lararia house shrine embedded into the wall.

Placing the flickering oil lamp delicately at the foot of the lararia, the mysterious figure slowly lowered their hood. Cascading locks of unkempt hair tumbled down around their weather-beaten countenance. Tilting his head upward, Arenius' seasoned eyes shimmered with a profound sense of contentment as he beheld the sacred shrine before him. The altar was not adorned with deities but instead depicted vibrant frescoes of Cornelius and Floriana in their youthful splendor. Captured in the heart of the mural, the two lovers stood face to face, their gazes locked in an intimate exchange as they intertwined their fingers. Against the backdrop of their hilltop villa, bathed in the golden glow of a painted sun, Cornelius and Floriana stood united, with azure peaks stretching into the distance beyond.

Arenius bends in a graceful arc, his movements fluid as he eases the weight of the traveling bag from his weary shoulder. Nestled beside it is Floriana's bow, known as The Banisher, a weapon of elegant craftsmanship. Gingerly, he places them on the ground before him. The bow, pristine despite its age, reminiscent of the day she unearthed it within the labyrinthine shelves of Alexandria's ancient library. With meticulous care, he unveils a mysterious object swathed in delicate linen, each fold whispering secrets of forgotten times.

"Ma, Pa. As promised, it is done," he vowed, laying a golden laurel beside the lamp, to have its flames reflected in the laurel's elegantly designed leaves. "After all our years and attempts, Susru no longer sits on the throne. Now you may rest. May The One light your path into Elysium."

Dirty streaks marked his weathered face as tears traced a path down his cheeks, carrying with them the weight of years gone by. With a solemn bow, he bid farewell to the flickering flame of the lamp, casting the room into a shroud of obsidian shadows once more.

Lost pages of Res Gestae Divi August

"I now hold unchallenged dominion over the Republic. The people of Rome will kneel, worshiping me as their god in flesh. Every deed I commit serves the cause, and none shall escape my judgment. Yes—we will seek out every Light Bringer and snuff them from existence. Yes, Lord Izraga, your return will be wrought through our hands, and the world will tremble before it."

paginae perditae factorum Divine Augustus
(Lost pages of the Deeds of the Divine Augustus)

Afterword

By his death in 14 AD, Gaius Octavius had assumed the name Augustus, and with it, he forged Rome into an empire, becoming its first emperor. Under his hand, the Roman Empire stretched to horizons the old Republic could scarcely imagine. Through a vast network of roads and the enduring peace he imposed, he laid the foundations of a realm destined to last for centuries. Augustus did not merely rule Rome—he embodied its spirit, its ambition, and its eternal glory.

About the Author

Also by Gary Winchester

As an author, I love to create a variety of worlds in which readers are able to get lost in. From post-apocalyptic earth to the furthermost galaxies, with tales of adventure and discovery in we as people can relate to.

First Encounter: A City of Silence Saga
A large chunk of the world's population was wiped out in the fires of a meteor shower that pummeled the surface. As the world cooled: Ice, famine, and disease took another portion. Now all that roams the planet are the survivors; the ones with the skill, grit, and intelligence to make it another day. On the frozen land, that was once known as England, battles are fought everyday between man and beast. To former mercenary Marcus Rowan, there is no distinction between the two. His team's survival is due to their ability to prepare and handle the worst man, and nature, can throw at them. However, when they arrive in London, Rowan and his team soon discover that they will not only encounter what survived the old world, but also what was born in the new world. Something more dangerous than anything they could have anticipated.

Don't Walk the Rails

In the shadowy outskirts of Baltimore City, a forgotten stretch of train tracks carries more than just rusted steel and fading memories— it carries a warning. They say if you walk the tracks after dark, *The Bunny Man* will find you.

For a group of thrill-seeking teenagers, it's just another urban legend—something to laugh about, something to challenge. Daring each other to prove it wrong, they venture out one night to explore the abandoned ACME Mattress Factory, a decaying relic perched alongside the rails. But what starts as a joke quickly turns into a nightmare.